a few tales later
A collection of short stories

by
CHRIS HICKMAN

To Claire & Sammy

Best wishes from Chris

Christmas 2017

Copyright © 2017 Chris Hickman

All rights reserved. This book or any portion thereof may not be reproduced or used in any manner whatsoever without the express written permission of the publisher except for the use of brief quotations in a book review or scholarly journal.

Cover design: Elaine Reynolds

First Printing: 2017

This book of short stories, compiled over 15 years is dedicated to dear friends, family, and daughters Lauren and Louise.

Thank you for your love.

Contents

Come Rain or Come Shine	9
My Interstellar Cosmic Washing Machine	15
Parlophone Sunset	19
The Shot	25
Lousey Diet	29
Devlin	33
Night Walking	37
The Blind Detective	43
Cambria Avenue on the Offensive	49
Postcard from the Past	55
Awkward Moment on Earth	59
Cramer House	65
Tormain Hospital	69
The Last Tourist	75
The Swirling Mist	79
Sam's Tale	85
The Playground	89
Mrs Norigi's Cat	93
The World is Richer	97
War Games	101
Histoire Parisienne	105
Oh Yeh!	113
The Snow Fox	119
Preston Gubbals has been Flattened	125

Continued

Mad as Hell	129
Flight of Fancy	135
I Never Thought It Would Come To This	141
In the Beginning was the Word	145
Café Crême	147
Dusty Old Book	151
Melangell	157
A Memorable Book	163
Bang You're Dead	168
The Captain's Bar	173
Puddle Jumping	178
A Classic Consultation	179
Blanked Out	185
Childhood Holiday	191
Cortez the Killer	195
Driving Thoughts	197
A Taste of Dickens	201
Five Sories on a Bus	207
Lost for a Moment in the Fantasy	215

Come Rain or Come Shine

Dinner is mostly taken early in Hollywood. Dawn make-up calls send the denizens of Beverly Hills, Bel Air, and Holmby Hills to their beds as the sun slips below the skyline.

On this night in 1941, the dinner guests leave the table and move from the formal dining room to the gathering room where they pour each other drinks, smoke, and consider who will be the first to occupy the baby grand opposite the fireplace.

Those present – stars and personalities every one – has been served scallopine of veal, boiled white rice, baked pared hubbard squash, coleslaw, whole-wheat bread, and a jellied coffee soufflé.

Apart from their celebrity status one other facet is inescapable – their youth. Mickey Rooney is barely 21, Judy Garland 19, singer and comic actress Martha Raye 25, Mel Tormé 16, and the hostess, singer Margaret Whiting, just 17.

Annie, the coloured maid appears as from nowhere, and from the top of the mezzanine steps announces in a quiet but audible voice that there is a telephone call. I call her Annie because she was one of a thousand Annies or Esthers, Sarahs or Hatties, who tidied up, kept house and kept schtum about the goings on in the Hollywood Hills. But that is not our story tonight.

Annie says: 'Phone for you Miss Margaret. It's uncle Johnny.'

'Thank you Annie. I'll take it in the kitchen.'

As Annie turns to leave she casts a censorious glance

towards the martini glasses and ashtray on the piano; a piano she dusted a few hours earlier.

Margaret returns a few moments later flushed with excitement.

'Johnny and Harold are coming up. They've got a new song they want us to hear. They wanted me to go over, but when I told them I had guests they insisted on rushing right over. They've literally just finished writing it. They think it will be big.'

Half an hour later, in walk two of America's greatest song writers, Johnny Mercer and Harold Arlen. And the song they brought with them is Blues in the Night. Arlen and Mercer have been working on the score for the film of the same name. It's a blues song scripted to be sung from a prison cell.

Margaret Whiting tells what happened next: 'They came in the back door, sat down at the piano and played the score of Blues in the Night. I remember forever the reaction. Mel got up and said, 'I can't believe it.' Martha couldn't say a word. Mickey Rooney said, 'That's the greatest thing I've ever heard.' Judy Garland said, 'Play it again.' We had them play it seven times. Judy and I ran to the piano to see who was going to learn it first. It was a lovely night.'

Harold Arlen said: 'The whole thing just poured out. And I knew in my guts, without even thinking what Johnny would write for a lyric, that this was strong, strong, strong! I went over his lyric, and I started to hum it over his desk. It sounded marvellous once I got to the second stanza, but that first twelve was weak tea'.

'On the third or fourth page of his work sheets I saw some lines – one of them was, 'My momma done tol' me, when I was in knee pants.' I said, 'Why don't you try that?' It was one of the very few times I've ever suggested anything like that to John.'

Margaret met Johnny Mercer and Harold Arlen through her father, himself a renowned composer. They are like family to her.

She recalls: 'I came home from school and was told my father was playing golf, and I decided to go down there. I took my bike – it was only two blocks – and I found him with five men, all of whom I knew. I said, "Hello Uncle Johnny." That was Johnny Mercer. "Hello Uncle Harry." That was Harry Warren. "Hello Uncle Harold." That was Harold Arlen. And then there was one man, much older than the rest of these people, who was kind of smiling about all this. And this man said, "I've heard about you, Margaret. I hear you're going to be a wonderful lady, and I've been anxious to meet you. I long for the day when you can call me Uncle Jerry. But right now I'm just Jerome Kern. So I said, "Gee, you're my father's favourite composer!" And the other three chimed in with, "OUR favourite composer".'

Uncle Johnny, 31, and uncle Harold, 36, keep a fatherly eye on Margaret. Her father died three years earlier at the height of his success.

But uncle Johnny is keeping more than a watchful eye on Judy Garland. He is besotted. A year earlier, when she was 18 they had become lovers. Even Hollywood considered the situation scandalous. To the dismay of friends, he had written in, 'That Old Black Magic', that she was:

"*The lover I have waited for*
The mate that fate had me created for."

The tensions around the piano this evening as they

introduce the song are subtle, but undeniable.

Judy is standing a little too close to Johnny at the piano; her hand on his shoulder. Occasionally her fingers brush the nape of his neck and he turns to smile the secret smile lovers share. Everyone sees.

Mickey Rooney, behind the boyish charm and the long drink, is wondering how, or if, he can ever pick up the pieces. He carries a deep and lifelong platonic love for Judy. They have already co-starred in several films, were a successful song and dance team, and received an Oscar nomination.

Judy is scarcely out of childhood. Only a year before she was starring as Dorothy in The Wizard of Oz. Mercer is a married man. Everyone is begging them to end the affair.

Across the piano, through the tobacco smoke, Martha Raye is twisting the wedding band around her finger, easing it over the knuckle and back.

And here our script becomes more entangled. Judy, while conducting a passionate affair with Mercer, is lining up Martha Raye's husband, David Rose, composer and orchestra leader. She becomes engaged and marries him this same year.

Thereafter Mercer's behaviour becomes increasingly unpredictable. He is captivated by Bing Crosby's hard-drinking circle, but also begins to hit the bottle at parties. This leads to vicious outbursts, contrasting markedly with his normal geniality.

He becomes a hideously mean drunk. Mercer denounces almost anyone within range. He even accuses Irving Berlin of lacking talent. However his long-suffering wife, Ginger is his most frequent victim.

Later in 1943 he writes, 'One for My Baby', which suggests that the relationship with Judy Garland is over.

In fact, they remain on-and-off lovers for decades. Three years later Mercer pens lyrics to Arlen's score for 'Come Rain or Shine'.

"I'm gonna love you like nobody's loved you
Come rain or come shine
High as a mountain and deep as a river
Come rain or come shine."

It's one of the greatest popular love songs of all time. And everyone around the piano this night will be in no doubt for whom it was written or what it's about.

"Days may be cloudy or sunny
We're in or we're out of the money
But I'm with you always,
I'm with you rain or shine."

Postscript

- Two days after Martha Raye was born, her mother was already back on stage. Martha first appeared in their act when she was three years old.

- When he was 14 months, unknown to everyone, Mickey Rooney crawled onstage wearing overalls and a little harmonica around his neck. He sneezed and his father, Joe Sr., grabbed him up, introducing him to the audience as Sonny Yule. His father was a womaniser and a drunk.

- Mel Torme first sang professionally at age four with the Coon-Sanders Orchestra, singing, "You're Driving Me Crazy" at Chicago's Blackhawk restaurant.

- Judy Garland's parents were vaudevillians who settled in Grand Rapids, MN, to run a cinema that featured vaudeville acts. With her two sisters she made her film debut in 1929. She was 12.

- Margaret Whiting was picked out for stardom at the age of seven. She was one of the first artists to be signed to Capitol Records. Margaret died January 10, 2011, aged 86.

• • • • •

My Interstellar Cosmic Washing Machine

That's the thing about washing machines... You tend to take them for granted until you need one. In my new state of independence I figured I could wash most of what I needed by hand. Then I needed a way to dry the items; the personals, the socks, the t-shirts, and the jeans.

Actually it was the jeans which tipped the balance. You can't wash them by hand – not in an apartment. Having dripping denim over the bath for a week or more is too depressing.

The other thing was that I was on an economy drive. My flat was more expensive than I planned. I had no garden – good thing and bad – my kitchen space was limited...

At first I looked at a hand-cranked machine for less than £40; suitable for caravans and campers. It would fit under the sink – perfect. I mentioned it to my mother on a visit. 'It sounds like a bit of a gimmick,' she said, and this from a woman with the onset of dementia. But she was right.

I allowed the purse strings to open a little wider and looked at twin tubs. Clearly I would need some kind of spin drier if I ever hoped to keep the bathroom free of wet clothes. I was also thinking about the plumbing involved. Getting in a plumber would add a minimum £100 to the bill.

Again the items available were suitable for students and mobile homes. It all seemed so temporary and I wanted more. In my heart I felt I hadn't many more moves left in me. Although the idea of hoses coming from kitchen taps and draining back into the sink was do-able, it was not ideal. My sisters knew this. I could see it in their eyes when I described the choices I was considering.

Finally I allowed myself to entertain the idea of a proper washing machine. I searched the internet for weeks. It must have been weeks? Finally I found the perfect model. She was reduced in price, of a make I approved, and they delivered free. This is important when you live up two flights of stairs.

My decision was bolstered when I read on the internet that the washing machine was probably the greatest invention of the 20th century. This was because it freed people, mostly women, to do other things. It freed them from trying to keep up with weekly laundry for six children and a husband. They had time to do better things, like go to the library.

And I thought about myself diligently wringing out socks and shorts by hand, and compared it to my new life in which my super new machine would wind up to 1,600 revolutions per minute forcing the last drop of surplus water from the garments, freeing me from household drudgery. I so wanted to be free of household drudgery.

It was then that a strange cross fertilisation of ideas occurred. I had been watching a TV programme which informed me that there exists a neutron star at the centre of the Crab Nebula. This is – please pay attention – a supernova remnant and pulsar wind nebula in the constellation of Taurus. It's about 6,500 light-years from Earth and at its centre is the Crab Pulsar, a neutron star or spinning ball of neutrons, 28 to 30km across.

This neutron star spins at 30 times a second, which is 1,800 times a minute – only 200 rpm faster than my washing machine's super spin cycle.

It occurred to me that if I could raise my spin cycle by just over six and a half revolutions a second, perhaps with the judicious use of some WD40, then I might be able to bend space time, in my kitchen. Yes, mass is a problem involved in these calculations I know, but wet jeans can be awfully heavy, particularly on a grey afternoon in late March.

The next revelation was even more astonishing and involved Mr Einstein. It appears that, according to his Theory of Relativity, the faster you travel the slower time moves. So someone zooming out into space and coming back will be chronologically younger than the people who stayed behind. I know it defies common sense unless you are a physicist, but they all maintain it's true.

Ergo my washing – stay with me here – must be getting newer every time I use my spin cycle. My washing is travelling at nearly the same speed as the surface of the Crab Pulsar. Think about it! One day I may open my super-large-vista washer door and take out my shorts brand new, still in their packet. My machine will pay for itself in no time – no pun intended.

I'm thinking of writing to the manufacturers because they might want to use this in their advertising. However, on second thoughts they may be purposefully keeping it a secret. Elderly persons might be tempted to rejuvenate by folding themselves into an extra-large deluxe model. It could be catastrophic – their colours might run and they could so easily pick the wrong cycle and come out even more crumpled than when they went in.

Then a metaphysical thunderbolt parked itself by my side. If Tibetans can use prayer wheels to beat their karmic debt simply by rotating a drum with the mighty mantra,

Om Mane Pedme Hung inside, then what might I achieve by placing the mantra in a plastic bag and sending it for a spin? I believe I could do quite a lot of catching up in relatively no time at all; pun entirely intentional. I could expunge – good word isn't it – the stains of past misdeeds even with a cool wash.

Thanks to my new washer, Nirvana has never been so close. Washday blues? That's such a cosmic joke.

· · · · ·

Parlophone Sunset

George Thorson stopped before the second-hand shop on his way back from the Citizens Advice Bureau. He had spent the morning struggling to comprehend an unwarranted slash to his pension.

Outside the shop was an orange box doubling as a display stand, and on it a stack of 78s. The top one caught his eye – Debussy's Clair de Lune. He set down his groceries, picked up the disc and eased it from the brown paper sleeve. He gently felt beneath for the centre hole and slid the disc further out. It looked good.

With groceries and record he entered the jumbled world of the New2U bazaar.

'How much,' he called, holding the prize aloft.

'Let me see," came the reply from behind a 42" plasma TV struggling for stability on a repro' roll top desk. 'Fifty pence, George, seeing as how you regularly spend "time"here.'

A smile tested George's lips. "Still want me to look at that job around back?"

'Soon as you like George. Knock this off the bill.' Mr New2U returned the record to George's gnarled hands, a builder's hands of more than 55 years.

Despite the offer, George fished out the 50p, snapped it on the counter, then made for home. It was starting to rain but George was smiling, inside at least.

The bus was on time. He held his pass on the card reader and ripped off the ticket that no–one ever checked.

During the ride home his unconscious took over.

Memories the record unlocked rehydrated from some arid corner of his mind, and he stepped again into the twilight living room – a particular room, a particular day.

Vera, his wife was seated before the window watching the retreating radiance in the sky. The gramophone was playing. It was Clair de Lune. He made to enter but with a simple motion of the hand she halted him. He stood at the door until the needle was sucked into its final endless orbit.

He thought she wiped away a tear, but then turned resolutely to face him. 'You'd better know George,' she said. Sometimes she could be brutally frank. 'I've been to the doctor. They think it's cancer. They think...'

George was across the room like a bullet. But in his haste he knocked the table and the stylus skudded across the record gouging an irreparable scar. Thereafter the piece always leapt abruptly to the end – rather like Vera's life.

The bus came to a halt. George stepped down and headed for the estate. As he reached the corner the usual gang of young reprobates was filling the space between the wall and a lamppost. What to do – walk in the gutter and show weakness, or go through the middle and risk trouble?

George was an elderly man, but he wasn't a weak one. He walked straight. His body was testament to years of labour. His hands were like undressed stone. For any of the youngsters a single clout would be enough. They parted reluctantly as he reached them.

'What you got Mr Thorson?' said the leader. 'You been shopping?'

'Hey lads. How you doing? Haven't you got homes to go to?'

'You been buying records Mr T'? I see you got somethin' special there.'

George's instinct was to draw his fragile find closer, but he resisted. Instead he held it out to the young man. 'I found it in the second hand shop. It's an old favourite.'

'That's cool man. I'd like to hear it.' A titter arose from some of the youths. They thought he was putting the old man on.

'Shut it you lot. It's music and music's good. You lot don't like that then be somewhere else.' He turned back to George, 'I would like to hear what that sounds like Mr Thorson.'

'Well I don't know...'

'I know where you live Mr Thorson. I could come round.'

George wasn't sure if this was a threat or a genuine request. He decided to risk it. 'OK Billy. It is Billy isn't it? You come round one afternoon.' With that he made his way up to his flat on the second-floor landing of Ackely Towers and locked the door behind him.

The next afternoon, as he was about to pour a cup of tea, the door bell rang. There was Billy. George was slightly shocked but recovered enough to invite him in.

'Do you want tea?'

'Sure,' Billy replied. 'Three sugars.'

Billy cast an eye over George's possessions. 'Nice place Mr Thorson. Nice and tidy – I like that.'

'Three sugars it is then.' When George returned from the kitchen he half expected an empty room, open door, and something missing from the sideboard. But no, Billy was sitting in George's chair with his feet up on the pouffé.

George handed over the tea then went over to an old record player, slipped the platter from its sleeve, blew on it in time-honoured fashion and set it on the deck. 'I'm not sure this is going to be your thing Billy. It's a long way from what people are listening to now.'

'Play the music Mr T'. Let's hear it.'

They both sat in silence as Claire de Lune filtered down from the past through pops and crackles, wobbles and hiss.

At the end George said: "What do you think? Was it worth the time?"

'That was very pretty Mr T'. Very lovely tune. It sounds special.'

'It reminds me of someone – my wife.'

'What happened?'

'She died. It was cancer. A long time ago now.'

'Bummer. It got my Auntie Gracie too. It don't seem fair.'

'That's the truth Billy. You hit the nail on the head. But how come you want to hear an old 78? What's going on?'

'Cause it's music man. It's like a universal truth.'

'Sorry?' George was stunned. He hadn't expected to wander into the realms of metaphysics this afternoon.

'I've been thinking Mr T'. Like, every generation has its music. It has its drug of choice and it has its music. Music for me it's like going to church. Maybe I pop a couple of E's, maybe I don't, but we dance. Every weekend tens of thousands of us dance – together. We don't fight, not on 'E's. We feel a connection, the love, and music is the key.'

'I'm afraid I don't agree with drugs.'

'I know you don't Mr T'. Your drug was booze, fags and ballrooms. In the 60s they smoked hash and listened to endless guitar impros' or bleedin' sitars with some guy beating shit out of the drums for 25 minutes. Victorians liked their laudanum. That's where this record is from.'

'I'm not sure about that Billy. They can't all have been high in those days.'

'Who knows.'

Billy placed his mug on yesterday's Daily Mirror.

'Well, I got places to be. Thanks for the tea. Let me know if you find any more good tunes. And don't get sad about your missus. Music can do that too sometimes.'

'You are right again Billy. Indeed you are.'

As the door closed on him George's solitude once more sealed the corners of the room like a grey fudge. Slowly the pattern disappeared from the wallpaper as twilight once more came to rest over Ackely Towers.

He wondered what Vera would make of his new acquaintance.

• • • • •

The Shot

Scene: At a village bus stop somewhere near Paphos. Katherine Harker, an elderly woman is alone except for the camera to which she is speaking.

It's strange. It's still so clear in my mind. Odd the way some things imprint themselves on your memory. I was standing in the top field. It was one of those autumn days when everything seems to have been tidied up. I remember looking at the field being ploughed on the other ridge and thinking how deep and brown the earth was; how straight and neat the furrows.

It was only mid afternoon but the rooks in the copse were preparing for the night ahead. There is always a lot of noise from them as they come back to the roost; to settle – a lot of caw cawing.

I had felt really happy that day. Everyone said the war would end in a few days – weeks at most. There would be time to get back to normal; an end to rationing – a period during which we would know it had all been worthwhile. I just wanted to stand there and breathe it all in.

I used to go up on the hill sometimes for a walk. I suppose it was to get out of the farmhouse. No matter what the weather I always felt as if my battery had been recharged. Sometimes the wind would blow clean through you. All the cobwebs went sailing away. Or the rain would wash you – sometimes soak you through, and you could come back fresh to everyday life, and fit right back in again – dry off, get warm by the stove and it was like no-one knew that you had been somehow renewed.

Of course in summer you went there and were warmed by the sun. I don't know if Everest is the top of the world but I felt I was on top of the world on days like those. Often the feeling was so strong I couldn't stand it for long. This day was different though. I had wrapped myself up and was just sitting watching the world turn. The clouds were broken and patches of sunlight moved across the valley. The rooks, I mentioned the rooks didn't I, were still squabbling in their rookery.

It's strange how noise carries on some days. Almost as if all the other sounds get turned down and you are just aware of one: a tractor, or the clanking from the dairy, or a dog barking somewhere far off. Just one sound, like the axe biting into a tree again and again. This day it was the rooks.

I had come up here the day Alan had gone off to join his regiment. There had been a bit of a send off over at his parents' farm.... I didn't go to the station. His brother, Thomas, drove him. I stayed a little while and helped with the clearing up. There was gallons of hot water and we were all being bright and cheerful, cracking jokes – even his old man managed a laugh – but we were just putting off the feelings inside. It is hard to see any young man, any mother's son, go off to fight. It is somehow even harder in the country. In those days many people had not travelled more than 15 or 20 mile except perhaps for the annual Sunday school outing when we motored off in a convoy to the coast for the day with a couple of pence to spend on brittle candy, fizzy pop or a ride on the cakewalk.

After we had cleaned up, as soon as I could, I slipped away and went up to my place on the hillside to sort of let it all out.

Thomas, I remember, was due for other things than the forces.

His feet kept him out of the army, his eyesight kept him out of the airforce and I just don't think the navy wanted him in any condition.

Anyway he found important things to do as an airwarden and also went around collecting all the metal fences from people's houses to make into bullets and guns. But that was later on when we were running a bit low on these things.

Some women were drafted into the Land Army. Well, it was no hardship for me – I was used to it. In fact it is a miracle they didn't send me off to some factory making aircraft and some other poor girl would have to learn about mucking out and planting crops. That was the sort of thing the authorities did in their almighty wisdom.

One girl I was at school with got sent to some secret sort of place to decode messages. I was glad I wasn't chosen. I'd've been homesick after the first night.

Anyway, there I am standing on my hill and I still had Alan's last letter in my pocket, just to read when I needed to. The wind dropped and in the distance, I remember, I could hear a car.

The rooks were silent now and there was just the sound of this little engine grinding up the lane towards the farm. Then I could see it. It was a blue Morris I think. For a moment it seemed lit up in the sunlight.

I don't quite know what was going through my mind then but I realised I was clutching the letter tightly – too tightly. I had almost screwed it up into a ball.

A cloud crossed the sun and suddenly from the copse, a shot rang out. The rooks started and flew up like black confetti in the wind, cawing and wheeling in a fresh gust. The second barrel went off – and I knew.

I knew at that very moment my Alan wouldn't be

coming back again. I knew that my life was, in a kind of way over and that no matter what happened after that it would never be the same.

It's funny how you know these things – so that when they gave me the news, I just nodded, there were no tears – not then at least.

Of course, I've had a good life since. I eventually married and we retired out here. Strangely enough, he worked at an aircraft factory making wings. It's been five years since he died. Sometimes I'm not sure whether to go back or stay. I know I would be glad to be able to go and stand on my hillside again. I think I'm in need of it.

· · · · ·

Lousey Diet

You know, I have to tell you, being a woodlouse is not as much fun as you might imagine. The diet...! The diet can be monotonous. Rarely anything fresh... However, between you and me, some of my kin are sampling something fresh – their own poo. Personally I've never developed the taste for it. To me it lacks, je ne sais pas... allure.

Decaying vegetable matter is pretty much what we woodlice are here for – our raison d'etre – eating rotting wood, and stuff. I love that word don't you – stuff?

We males aren't even needed for rumpy pumpy. Females, like Candice over there, can get pregnant on their lonesome. It's unspeakably depressing. It makes me want to binge – binge, binge, binge on more rotten, rotting wood.

But, one's truly irrepressible nature must always shine through. 'Candice! Listen darling:'

"Oh Candice my love,
I hold all your 14 segments dear.
Sometimes I like to watch you from the rear,
When you spray your amonia lotion,
In one wiggly woggly motion,
Grooving from all your many hips
Come be my love, and munch some more wood chips."

Deaf as a post that one.
We used to be aquatic you know, in times gone by. Now... ...well, not so much....

One or two have returned to water, become

submariners. They seem to prefer the company of shrimp and the like. Perhaps that's why we adore dampness. It's a hereditary thing.

While I have your ear I have to say that you people can be a bit of a nuisance. You come stomping around turning up our bits of bark and our snuggly rocks. All that nonsense about being animal lovers... Certainly not crustacean lovers. Those you aren't eating, you're squashing. Well don't come round here trying to pick a fight. You'll get more than you bargained for I can tell you. There are more of us than you. Forty five different types in UK alone – five of them common. I detest that word – 'Common'. Who's common for heaven's sake?

'Hello Deidre. You look captivating today. Lovely configuration – no, really lovely.' Three thousand different types of us around the world. And what have you people got, I ask you? Well no, I don't know either.

I have to say I am still trying to lose weight. Shedding a layer of exoskeleton is quite a pfaff. I'm making this one last. It's not that easy. I've tried most of the diets.

Atkins diet; a bit too meaty for me. Cambridge Diet; Food Combining – or are they the same thing? Pal-E-O; Cabbage Soup... That one wasn't too bad to be honest. I could paddle around in that for days.

I've munched on grapefruit, once it rotted down. I even nibbled on some pineapple. I've had a go at controlling my pH balance; toyed with pro-biotics; attempted to get a handle on my sugar consumption; tried to cut out fat.

I don't really see that much fat.

Watch out! Here comes Rowena. God she's hot. 'Hello Rowena darling. Can I help you with that lovely lump of mulch you've found?

It looks far too heavy for svelt little you.

And the same to you sweetheart. No, you roll yourself into a ball why don't you.'

That's what you get for trying to be nice. Clearly someone's been drumming on her back all night – hussy! It's not as if there's a mulch shortage. Mulch to the far distant horizon.

Oh, there goes Gwen. Look at the sheen on her cuticle. Like she'd just stepped out from beneath a patch of dry rot. Sorry but I need to catch her before dance class. She's in the regional dance-off with a very compelling piece. Her rumba, let me tell you, is something else.

'Gwen... Gwen darling... Anything I can help you with? No...' Apparently not.

You know there just isn't the same sense of community there used to be. We were such a gregarious crowd. Back in the day we would all muck in. Woodlice families from all backgrounds getting stuck in. It's so different now. My analyst says I'm not to dwell on these things, but what can you do?

Of course there are times I've asked myself – haven't we all – 'What's the point? What's it all for? Is it worth going on? If I, "went" who would care? No-one.' Those are the dark days. Sometimes I don't eat – anything. And what's life without eating? Who was it said, I eat therefore I am?

Leslie! Have you got a minute? Leslie darling, I've got that book you were asking... She's always on the go that one. Never still for a minute. That seems to be the key; to keep busy, keep going. Sometimes I look at all the scurrying around me.... I look...

I look out from some well of deep sadness and wonder, 'Are they all just keeping going?

Of course I make the effort to involve myself. There's

bridge club on Thursdays. We take it in turns to host the evening... Put on a little supper afterwards. It's mostly wood. I don't partake. It's not that I don't trust them, but preparation is everything you must agree.

Then there's choir on Tuesday evenings. We're just learning a new song to add to our repertoire – 'You Raise Me Up'. There's an acapella solo at the start which Jean is taking, when her marsupium heals. Shouldn't be too long now.

I know – come to the opening concert on the 15th. I'll find you tickets, but let me know ASAP because they are going like you know what. It should be a night to remember.

Claris! Can I see you for just one minute. Claris dear, No don't run away sweetheart.

· · · · ·

Devlin

It was mid-November, and a day when nature contrives to kill you. Mountainous waves exploded against the sea wall. Along the esplanade an icy fusillade of rain sliced to the bone.

I had been walking for forty minutes and seen only one brave couple huddled in a Victorian shelter with Tuperware sandwiches and a large Thermos – making the best of it. Ten minutes later I spotted him, crouched on the steps of the old Odeon. He looked all in. It was only when I had nearly passed he monotoned: "Spare some change please." More of a demand than an appeal.

I was about to pass when, for reasons unknown, I stopped and asked: "Want some tea?"

He considered for a moment then, gathering his sleeping bag and other paraphernalia, joined me along the prom'. There was one café open. It felt like the last on the planet. The windows dripped with condensation and the floor was awash from discarded rainwear. I ordered tea and toast. He ate it – all. I ordered more. He ate that too. Eventually conversation seemed appropriate. He said his name was Devlin. The whole tawdry history followed. I wasn't really listening to any of it. Basically he'd plunged into the trap of homelessness. No home, no address, no state support, no income – no future…

Don't ask why but I suggested he might be temporarily accommodated in the studio I had built in my garden. I liked to call it a studio but really it was a large shed with a decent window. I thought he might quote my house as his postal address and claim benefit. He could use the back gate to come and go, so he need never venture in the house. I don't understand why I asked him. I rarely take anyone home since my mother died. I set a few ground rules: no lodgers, no pets, no mess and it was tacitly agreed. Then like a wet dog he followed me home and surveyed what was to be his new abode.

With a curt nod of approval I was dismissed. Next day I found all my art materials on the back doorstep.

Things were alright at first. He signed on and I placed his gyros under a stone by the art room door. He came and went via the rear, and to be honest was no trouble at all.

Then one day I caught sight of a stranger furtively wrestling with the back gate which stuck in the wet. From then on I became more attentive and saw more strangers popping in and out. It got worse. My neighbour complained that his vegetable patch was being defiled. That's the only word I can use as gardening was to him more of a calling than a hobby.

I determined to speak firmly to Devlin. He promised things would improve. They got worse. Neighbours on both sides complained of petty thefts, litter and faeces; and they all were pointing the finger at me and my lodger.

So I took the bull by the horns and told Devlin he wasn't welcome and to clear off back to the sea front. By now the weather was as good as it gets on our bit of coast. I gave him £50 and told him to leave and never return. He laughed. He laughed that patronising laugh when people perceive what they believe is an idle threat. I took it as a challenge. Next day I bagged his belongings by the back gate and got Hired Hands (We do what you don't want to) to disassemble the shed, break up the concrete base and remove the lot while he was out panhandling.

I was expecting trouble and I was right. Devlin stormed through the kitchen door, grabbed me by the neck and produced a wicked looking blade from beneath his parka. He was crazy. His eyes were wild and his speech almost incoherent. However he left me in no doubt that I was to rebuild his hut and he would be moving in with me until I had accomplished it. There was also the codicil that he would have anyone to stay he damn well liked.

I called him ungrateful, freeloading scum. His face became a mask of hatred. He nicked me with the raw blade behind the ear then punched me hard in the gut. I went down, doubled over in pain. Then he did it. He spat in my ear. The scum spat in my ear.

You've heard of the red mist overtaking people, well that was pretty much what it was like. As he turned to leave I climbed to my feet and swung a heavy cast-iron skillet from the stove in a wide arc catching him at the side of the head. As he dropped like a stone he caught his temple on the corner of a kitchen unit.

I wasn't surprised he was dead. A curious elation swept over me. I felt wonderfully alive. My mind clicked into overdrive and my course of action seemed clear, almost as if I had planned everything from the start.

After a nice cup of tea I stripped him and placed his filthy clothes in a bin bag to leave outside the charity shop. I dragged the corpse to the chest freezer in the garage and made room within.

Next day my disposal plan was put in motion. I bought a large kennel and had Hired Hands build a small pen. Then I collected a beautiful German Shepherd pup and determined to build her up on prime cuts of Devlin.

Of course I have seen enough CSI programmes and

know that the long bones, pelvis and skull are always the hardest to dispose of.

After my hungry pup, Eva, had got through Devlin's left leg I called Hired Hands again. They errected a workshop where the art room had been. I ordered flat bed saws and other interesting-looking tools and began cutting Devlin's femur into handy lumps. As the winter storms arrived again I would walk Eva along the front and from time to time toss a handful of fragments into the shingle along the beach where nature ground them away.

Now Devlin is finished I have cleaned the tools and sold them on Ebay. The shed was advertised in a local paper two counties away. The reasonable price and offer to deliver gave me a quick sale. It has all turned out a nice little project for the year.

The other day as Eva led the way along the prom, the wind whipping at our coats, she paused and sniffed the breeze. Then I heard the demand, 'Spare some change please'!

· · · · ·

Night Walking

The guests had left hours before. With his help, his wife had cleared the detritus of the evening, stacked the dishwasher and put out the empties.

She had taken herself off to bed. He remained with the choice of several malts and some old jazz playing out the stubbornly resistant, but abysmally small, fire in the inglenook.

It was hard to identify the moment, but he became acutely, and morosely, overwhelmed by the futility of his life. The usual stringy questions arose. Was it always going to be like this? What was the point? Could he reconnect with his life story – the one he dreamed up long ago?

Ben the black Lab' nudged his hand; his whisky-filled hand. Time for a walk. Time for both of them. He didn't drain his glass. He liked to have the remains of drinks around the house so that were he to misplace his glass, he might re-discover one he'd left earlier.

Ben was psychic. Like most dogs he knew when he was going out. His time. His time to thrash about in the darkness while his master – master, that was a laugh – ambled down to the bridge over the tiny river along the lane.

Dragging on his coat and wellingtons, he grabbed the dog's lead and a torch, then as he opened the back door, Ben careered out into the blackness like a soul possessed.

Ben was not one of those dogs that will walk to heel all day. He was no, slow, black, sloe black Labrador bobbing dog. He was a dog with a mission. There was ground to cover.

It had snowed the day before but now there was frost in the air, a stringent icy coldness that scored his nasal passages. He halted by the gate and breathed in the stillness.

Sometimes the darkness is full of foreboding. On other occasions one is part of it. One is part of what's out there, something of the unknown, a piece of the blackness. He took some moments to measure what this night would be, friend or foe.

Ben broke through the hedge from the field then dived back through on the opposite side of the lane. The field on the left was too wet for anything but grazing. On the right, a coppice with mixed, broad leaves on the perimeter. Deeper in were avenues of dark pine. The hedge wasn't well kept – in fact it wasn't kept at all. No point – nothing was worth protecting. And tonight everything was wrapped in a snowy coverlet.

He trudged on down the lane, listening, listening for Ben's whereabouts, and for other sounds. Tonight had the muffled ambience that accompanies a snowfall. Only the crunching of his boots and Ben's sporadic rampaging back to regroup were evident.

Three quarters of the way to the bridge he paused checking once more his place in the still night's scheme. Years before he had needed to leave the countryside to grow as a person. On returning home he was surprised, and comforted, to find himself attuned to the landscape at some deep level. He found himself endowed with some other kind of knowing, mysterious, unspeakable, almost pagan.

He gave himself up to the feeling, and stepped from the lane through the curtain of trees and into the woods. It felt like submerging in a secret pool.

Again he paused, letting the night's message filter through. The torch was in his hand but turned off. Night vision was enough in this moonlit snow-dressed landscape. A torch alerts anyone, or thing, to your presence long before you see them.

Carefully he pressed through the woods, skirting the impenetrable younger pines until he came to a broader avenue he recognised. He began to follow it into the heart of the woodland still wary of what else might be about. But what else could be? Reason told him nothing.

Then he heard something – something real. It was ahead; a rambling shuffling noise. What? What could it be? He froze, his heart doubling then tripling its pace. The mind races through possibilities: poachers, criminals, a coven even.

Gathering courage he trod carefully forward, trying not to reveal himself. He made himself vary his gait. Nothing in nature is regular, or so he'd been told. Eventually he could make out in the clearing ahead a shape low down, near the woodland floor. It was large enough to be a person. Crazy.

Out here in the middle of the night, in the middle of the wood, a person on hands and knees..?

He flicked on the torch. The beam cut the frosty night and revealed a boar – a wild boar for heaven's sake. Both boar and human were startled. The animal recovering its purpose more quickly than he, continued snuffling along the ground ahead. As he stared in disbelief the animal raised its eye and glowered. It was a look of disdain, of arrogance.

Perhaps it was the alcohol; perhaps the fact that here were two most unlikely creatures to be found in the middle of this woodland at this time of night but the absurd idea to mentally project a feeling of harmony to the animal occured to him.

It was a shock when the words, 'What on earth do you think you are trying to do?' were clearly returned in his brain. A strange aberration, a psychotic break, too much whisky fuelling an overactive imagination..?

The boar continued rummaging around in the snow-covered soil. The eye still holding him in view.

He recovered just enough to return the response, 'And what do you think you are doing'?

'Looking for the meaning of life,' came the boar's retort. 'While you on the other hand are just searching for sustenance, depite appearance to the contrary.'

'What do you mean?'

The boar ignored him. He asked again – and again.

Finally the animal raised his head and piercing him with that baleful look said: 'You don't belong here tonight. This is not your time to be here'. With that it turned and shambled into the darkness.

For a full minute he stood rooted, trying to assemble the muddle of feelings. It had happened. Certainly the animal had been there.

There were footprints to prove it. As for the rest...

Ben careered into view and explored the territory, nose down spunging in the boary aroma. After a sortie around the clearing the dog seemed strangely disinclined to pursue it further. They went home.

Days later in the pub, not with some little trepidation, I raised the subject of wild animals in the woods. One of the older locals confided, 'Oh, you've seen 'im too eh? Canny ol' bugger inna 'ee?'

He tugged his ear and grinned, then fixed him across the bar with a look he felt sure he'd witnessed before.

• • • • •

The Blind Detective

A large German Shepherd Dog guided Alan Gordon into the interview room and around the periphery of the table where Marcus Pagett slouched. From the corner DC Bill Browning raised his baleful glance from the prisoner only fleetingly.

'Mornin' boss.' He reached for the recorder and formally announced: 'DI Gordon enters the room.'

Pagett stirred to watch Gordon and the dog. 'They allow bloody animals in here now?'

Gordon dropped the harness and walked unfalteringly to the reinforced window and the narrow shelf covering the radiator. He rested both hands on it then turned directing his sightless gaze towards the prisoner.

'She's just my guide dog, Marcus. Don't worry about Jess.'

The dog inclined its head expectantly then lay at the edge of the room, muzzle on paws; eyes alert.

Gordon stepped confidently in the direction of the table, extending his hand for the edge; a routine he had practised. On this occasion he misjudged and kicked the table leg causing him to rapidly adjust balance and composure. He felt for the chair back and seated himself in one fluid motion. Pagett moved back.

'Well Marcus, you have been busy.'

'It's a fit up and you know it.'

'Marcus I'll start in the middle and save time. Your alibi's a lie. We found your DNA at the scene. We even recovered stolen goods from your gaff, so cut the crap. Oh yes! And there was that other thing – the girl's body.'

Marcus' knuckles whitened. 'It's a lie. I never hurt anyone...'

The dog shuffled nearer Pagett's chair.

'What happened Marcus? She catch you raiding her grandfather's shop?'

'I told you I never...'

'It'll go easier if you tell us,' Browning chipped in. 'I can see how it might have happened. She caught you unawares. You lashed out. It was an accident.'

Pagett glanced uneasily between them.

DI Gordon was patting his jacket as if searching for something but then slammed his palm on the table top. 'Except, Marcus, you didn't have to fiddle about. There was no need to molest the body of that poor girl – except you couldn't help yourself. Nice lithe Asian girl... Bit of forbidden fruit...'

Pagett flushed. He pushed back his chair and made to stand. Jess was next to him in an instant and sat with one large paw conspicuously on Pagett's grubby loafer. He withdrew his foot but Jess replaced her paw immediately.

Recovering his cool he looked insolently into the blind eyes of DI Gordon. 'Fuck you,' he mouthed. What Gordon missed, Jess hadn't. The dog surveyed him like a wolf reviewing breakfast. A persuasive set of industrial-size teeth was starting to show.

Low, disdainful growls came from her throat.

There was a knock and the duty sergeant entered. 'Pagett's brief is here.'

'Show him in', Gordon replied. Jess retreated to her spot.

The young lawyer marched in and exchanged a few whispered words with the suspect. 'I would like more time to confer with my client.'

'Interview terminated at 10.33,' Browning stated. Jess moved to DI Gordon's side and together they left the room.

Browning went to collect tea and placed the boss's mug on his desk. After Jess had nudged Gordon more than once he rummaged in one of the drawers and produced a tired Rich Tea biscuit which she accepted delicately in her front teeth. Then it was gone in one. A tongue like wet leather swept the extremities of her mouth.

'Can we get Pagett to cough, boss? We have 'circumstantial' but it would help if he pleaded.' Gordon patted his jacket searching for cigarettes he had long ago renounced.

'Have you noticed how protective he is of his personal space? Like most 'scallies' he hates people crowding him. I think we will do just that. Just a little more pressure and who knows...'

Forty five minutes later they were back with Pagett and his lawyer.

'My client, Mr Marcus Pagett, will admit to the burglary at Pindal's Asian supermarket on October 15.

'However he wishes to make clear he was in no way responsible for the death of Samantee Pindal.'

'Oh Marcus...' Gordon felt across the table as if searching for something. As he neared Marcus' hand he heard him withdraw it. 'What are we going to do? It looks bad.'

Jess returned to Pagett's chair sandwiching him between the lawyer. An emboldened Pagett leered: 'Has that mutt farted. It smells terrible. Can't you leave it outside?'

DI Gordon raised his nostrils. 'To the contrary, it is you who stinks. Jess smelt you first. She picked you out in that 'greasy spoon'. She remembered your scent from the 'scene' and Browning here had the wit to notice when you bolted. That's why we brought you in. But now I can smell it. I can smell your fear; I can smell the piss on your trousers; I can smell the donner kebab you ate last night and I can smell your guilt.'

Pagett was sweating. Jess moved closer, her lip quivering in a struggle to control a full-on snarl. She began making urgent, throaty noises.

Pagett's lawyer cut in. 'I must ask you to keep your dog under control Inspector.'

'Jess!' Gordon paused, 'I wonder if your client would mind if I touched his face?'

Pagett's expression said, 'What?' and his solicitor looked momentarily nonplussed. 'I would like to explore Mr Pagett's face to get a mental picture – if he would be so kind.'

After a few whispered words the lawyer said: 'Make it quick.'

Gordon stood but deliberately made a hash of it. The chair clattered noisily onto its back. Jess moved forward but Gordon bid her stay. She sat ears pricked, nose glistening; eyes watchful for the merest wrong move.

As Gordon started off again he caught his foot on the table leg and stumbled towards the radiator. He caught himself before he hit the deck but rose hands outstretched. Slowly turning he began to shamble towards Pagett, arms ahead; hands searching in his blackness.

Inexorably he groped nearer. With each step the

prisoner grew more uncomfortable. The groping, blind hands felt forwards, heading directly for him. Gordon's blind eyes rolled in that terrible unseeing manner and the hands... The hands fumbled ever nearer.

'Keep off, keep off! Get him a-fucking-way from me,' he mewled.

Pagett had virtually retreated to his lawyer's lap.

When Gordon was within a foot Pagett made to bale backwards but there was a deafening bark and Jess blocked his exit.

'Get off. I didn't mean it. It was an accident.'

Browning cut in, 'Did you kill Samantee Pindal?'

'I didn't mean to hurt her.' Just... Don't paw me.'

'Did you kill her?'

Gordon was within millimetres of Pagett's face. His soft, white fingers probing forward.

Jess barked again.

'Yes, he yelled Yes! Just don't let him touch me.'

· · · · ·

48

Cambria Avenue on the Offensive

Those mornings... Remember them? All you had to do was get up; down breakfast, and get out to meet the boys. I suppose it must have been summer. I seem to remember I was wearing an airtex shirt and khaki shorts – fairly standard issue for a boy still at primary school.

The idea was to get out and down my road as fast as possible, then meet up outside Danny's house in the Avenue. We were the Cambria Avenue Gang. In fact someone else called us that. We never thought of ourselves as a gang – more a club. We also didn't really want any of the warlike attributes connected with the Grove Gang or the Town Gang to be associated with us. Most of the time, we tried to keep out of their way in case they thought we wanted to claim their territory. That would be an act of aggression and could lead to unthinkable hostilities. Men could be captured if they wandered too far into the other's territory, and then there could be torture perhaps, or an afternoon's imprisonment and questioning behind the garages. What on earth could we tell them? Our passwords? We already knew who was on our side and who on theres'.

Nevertheless, I recall we did line up for war on one, possibly two occasions. The first is still fresh in my mind after all the years. You had to round up everyone you knew, to swell the numbers on your side. Inevitably some of the conscripts were too young to understand the gravity of the battle about to occur. These poor unfortunates would be sucking sweets or, 'having to go home for Rusks or something else. Mostly, those that willingly joined up for the fray, were just pleased to be included.

We, the core members, on the other hand, were deadly serious. It was uncharted territory for most; although we always spent a lot of time fashioning weapons, clubs, bows and arrows, shields, medieval stuff like that; and we practised for the day we would have to use these implements. Suddenly the reality that the bullies in the Grove Gang were going to knock our blocks off became truly scary.

We held a war council and talked in low tones about tactics, and where the field of battle should be. Some neutral character, with a bike, cycled back and forth between the two forces relaying messages and sometimes reporting on strength, attitude or morale of the other side.

It was decided that the two forces would engage on the pitch behind the new houses at 2pm. It was a schedule that allowed everyone time to go home for lunch. The temptation to stay home was great. However, no self-respecting Cambria Avenue member could come back next day with an excuse that his mum had kept him in. You had to turn up, even if it meant being severely wounded.

I gathered my weapons, and with some dignity left the house for a war I had never wanted. Some of my comrades were already assembled in the Avenue, The die-hards had turned up. Phil, Danny, Pop, Cheesy, Robin, Malcolm; Olli I think... There were sundry others, whose fighting skills would be negligible but it was good to have the numbers.

The bike kid came back with news that the enemy were assembling. We decide to move up to the battle field in loose formation. We thought about choosing a scout but the bike kid said he would go, so everyone was happy to let him.

Our safest entry, would be via Beech Drive. Other options took us either into their territory, or through the chain fence around the small filter beds on the outskirts of the new houses. The latter was a difficult route and would leave us tired, scratched and probably nettled before we even met the enemy.

When we arrived, there had obviously been some misinformation. We were the first there. The bike kid said he would go off and tell the Grove Gang that we had arrived. I remember, it was hard to feel grateful to him. He on the other hand seemed cheerfully willing – even eager to go. Half an hour later they arrived, the Grove Gang, and we drew up our lines, crouching behind our homemade shields, but not so close that you could see the whites of any of their eyes.

Perhaps they had more than us, but not too many more. And actually, they didn't look that fierce. Perhaps some of the "A" team couldn't make it that day. It was actually fairly interesting to see who had collected in their ranks instead of ours. There were people over there that I thought were – if not my friends – at the very least not Grove Gang material. Some were from the other side of town and shouldn't have been there at all by rights. I surmised that they probably turned up to play 'footie' or something and got conscripted.

We settled down to see what would happen. There followed a fairly intense period of waiting and muted discussion. Oh, and a lot of staring. The tension mounted. If anything was going to happen it would be soon; after all we all had to get home for tea, and some foot soldiers actually had tea at 4.30, and went to bed while it was still daylight.

There was a movement in the ranks, and one of their

lieutenants walked forward carrying a stick with a white hanky tied to the top. Quickly, one of our junior officers was elected to go out and meet him in no-man's land. All of us had been designated a rank. I am not sure by what criteria the elections were made, but if you didn't like the rank you were given, you just ignored it.

The two envoys moved out under the flags of truce and from my position, what seemed to be ensuing was a fairly amiable, but brief, conversation. Our man returned and reported that their leader was asking for a, 'parley'.

I think there was a moment of uncertainty in our commander-in-chief's face, as he stood and looked down at us. Still, it was only a moment, and I can forgive him that.

He entrusted his weapons to his second-in-command, and with only one rearward glance and a sigh of resignation, moved to meet the Grove Gang leader.

We strained our ears but could hear nothing. Nor could we tell how things were going by the body language. The future of the whole area was balanced on this moment. Reputations would be made and lost; future protocols would be set; no-go areas defined; and enemies and allies marked, if not for the foreseeable future, then the remainder of the summer at least.

Eventually our man turned and began to walk back. 'What happened?' We all wanted to know what was going to happen. Solemnly we gathered around.

"We have signed a truce," he declaimed. "The battle is off."

I actually heard one or two express regret. As I looked up, the opposing army was already dispersing. Someone from the other side shouted to one of our men about meeting on the school field for a game of football.

Normality was quickly flooding back in. The heightened state of alert sank like a soufflé.

We slowly ambled back to base camp in the Avenue, chewing over the events, and exaggerating where we could, anything worth the re-telling.

When I arrived home that evening, I was not unhappy to lay down my arms. Tomorrow would be a new day, and with the day there would be new expeditions. Tomorrow was going to be a day to explore new territory.

· · · · ·

Postcard from the Past

How strange that this sense memory should come to him now. It was a sour, bitter flavour that coated his soft palate. Something like laurel – the crushed leaf of a laurel – but no... Something... Something else – walnuts, fresh off the tree, and others lying there in the leaves – some of their hard green casings beginning to rot into a dye that stained everything: hands, clothes, everything, tobacco brown. The spoils of war. The stains of glory. The fruits of the earth found and recovered. A small bounty for a schoolboy.

He gave his mind freedom to investigate the postcard thrown up by memory. The afternoon was grey. It was autumnal but dry. Trees were still shedding the summer's leafy abundance. Now there was only the chastening caress of winter in prospect. He inhaled it. Even after all these years he could summon up the phantom of his childhood, and particularly this day after school with his pal Harry and two hours of boyhood liberty before tea.

Harry thought they should look behind the WRVS building on the corner. It was never open. You could sit on the flights of red tiled steps and still see over the balustrade – people, cars, lorries full of rattling churns... No-one minded two small boys. It was close to Harry's house. His mum had warned him not to go far because he would be called soon. So it was decided.

How strange then... What a shock. Yes it was a real shock to find that two older boys were already there. Harry knew one of them. It was probably going to be alright. He remembered the moment of fear. Would there be trouble? It seemed not. One boy propped his bike against the hedge. There was a passageway leading to some gardens beyond the building. It wasn't often used. There was a tall, dark privet hedge to the side bordering the cottage hospital, and an old chain-link fence on the other, protecting the gardens. They'd never thought to explore it before. It only led to a dead end.

There was talk of a plan, a plan to get walnuts – but there was a problem. The tree was in an old man's garden at the end of the passage and someone had to crawl under the fence. The big boy was – well, too big he explained. It had to be the two younger ones. And then amid the anxiety of the act, the trespass, the fear of capture, the deal was laid out. For every two walnuts collected, they could keep the next for themselves.

The arrangement was agreed. It had been more of a command by the older boy than a suggestion. Another recollection intermingled. It was of the bulky but boundlessly graceful Oliver Hardy berating Stan for, "Another nice mess you've got me into". Here was a situation. It was uncomfortable. He weighed the odds of being caught, against backing down. No-one wants to go through school tagged a coward thereafter, avoiding certain people and places. He checked the garden again. It didn't look as if anyone ever went there.

Not easy getting under the fence even with the big boy raising it as high as he could. The wire scraped along his back. If he got too dirty, or tore his clothes he would be in hot water. The older boy's mate left. He had decided that there were other fish to fry and jerked the front wheel of his cycle off the ground as he made a show of tearing away to some new, more demanding exploit.

So now there remained the three in the fading light and two on the wrong side of the fence furtively scrabbling among dry and dusty leaves for the sticky, brown rewards.

They gathered everything they could and split for home. When his father got in from work the boy proudly displayed the spoils to his mother and him. As he held out the dark brown mess in his hands to his mother and father, he noticed the smile that crossed his father's lips as he told of the deal arranged by the big boy. It was then, at that moment, he saw how he had been snared. It took longer for him to grasp how he had been manipulated. It took years in fact.

The postcard of the scene would revisit his memory from time to time. As he grew older it seemed smaller, less detailed and he would need to work harder to pour the colour back in. But once he had it, he could walk around in the memory as if it were yesterday.

In the kitchen, he remembered, there were more smiles exchanged between his parents as they watched him discover that he couldn't simply wash away the walnut stain. The few walnuts he had brought home now seemed hardly worth the effort, risk or mess.

Over the coming weeks as the discolouration on his hands slowly disappeared, he reflected on how he had been so easily led to such an unfair adventure. Chewing a pencil in class, he would return to his exercise book and catch sight of the stain. Playing marbles in the playground... Washing for dinner...

The stains stubbornly remained for weeks.

Even today his innocence still stung him momentarily in the recollection, before he smiled for himself. He had learned to do that much. He had learnt a few more lessons since that day.

The postcard in his memory sank back in time. He drew

two deep breaths and moved to close the curtains. Beyond the window the light was fading. Another fantastic sunset thanks to pollution. As he reached to switch on the table lamp in his study he was aware that he might need a drink – something to take the edge off the day. Something to lay the ghosts. Spirit on spirit. He drew the cork from the Cragganmore and was almost surprised to see there were no stains on his hands. Of course there weren't.

• • • • •

Awkward Moment on Earth

Awkward, yes, that would describe the breakfast, although I find myself searching for something less euphemistic. Until last night, my sojourn on your little planet had been going well, and for some months.

I had taken lodging with the family who now sat around the table with me in various states of distress. Last night my People Pack packed in half way through Emmerdale, and I was revealed as what must have seemed an unthinkably hideous creature, a creature beyond their imagination or comprehension.

The only one who appeared at all relaxed about the situation, to which I will come, was the son, 13-year-old Donny who had just offered me second dibbs on the fried bread. The grandmother watched with a baleful eye as far from the table she could sit. The father, Eddie was just staring into his lap – I had restrained them all with a little immobiliser device provided for just such an occasion – and the mother, Josie, was on the edge of some kind of psychotic break.

I was unintentionally responsible for this because one of my feeder tentacles had acted as it normally would, and had simply gone for the alpine muesli near her, in preference to the bacon, plum tomatoes, mushrooms and fried egg in front of me. Feeder tentacles have, pretty much, a mind of their own. They detect a food source and select the optimum requirements for my sustenance. I say me, but me and my various body parts usually work as a team.

There was silence in the room, except for Josie's

blubbing. After my Pack failed I put an isolation cape over the property. It's not the easiest thing to get right on a council house owing to the proximity and unpredictability of the neighbours.

Now I had the family's attention at the breakfast table I thought I should venture an explanation.

'Why is a bubble round?' They looked at me in horror and disgust. I re-tuned my Speech Patterniser and tried again. Their dismay changed to incomprehension. I gave them a moment to ponder, and then continued: 'Because it is the perfect shape for this environment. You are your perfect shape for here.'

'Warrington?' Donny threw in.

'No Earth; planet Earth.'

'Cool'.

'Where I come from this shape you see is the best for me. It's evolution.'

'You want to get back to where you came from,' Granny spat from behind the Coco Pops. 'Coming here, taking people's jobs; scaring everyone to death. I didn't live through the Blitz to have things from the arse end of nowhere come and infest our living room.

Eddie butted in: 'It's my living room, Mum, well Josie's and mine. You just live here.'

I could see we were drifting off track to one of their deeply felt, but repetitive subjects of engagement.

'Well you see, I have just been living here to see how you all get on with life.'

'You are from another planet then?' Donny asked.

I was fascinated by his apparent acceptance of the situation. Then I realised it probably came from hours battling for and against other life forms on his X-box.

'It is more of a dimensional thing, Donny.' You see there are more dimensions in existence than you can actually experience here. You see three and also are affected by time, but there are eleven, at least eleven important ones to us all. But that doesn't mean some things are in one dimension, and some in another...'

I could see I was losing them. 'It's like Narnia.' They looked blank. 'The story about the lion the witch and the wardrobe?' Still nothing. 'The children go through the back of the wardrobe and find a whole different world there.'

'Well why don't you piss off back there,' Granny hissed.

Josie let out an enormous sob which seemed to rouse Eddie. He had tried to do the manly thing and evict me from the settee last night, but had soon realised that he was desperately out of form when it came to scrapping with intergalactic travellers.

'Why us?' he asked. 'Why do you want to come and look at us'?

I had to tread carefully here. Even though I was going to bleach their memories, it is still possible to leave indelible scars which become generational mutations.

You only have to look at people's irrational fear of snakes – and spiders, for that matter.

'Well you are very interesting because you are so unaware. In your culture you always portray aliens as powerful beings ready to destroy mankind. But consider...'

I paused to collect my thoughts.

'There are inhabitants on some worlds for whom your saliva and skin oils would be ultra corrosive. The sound from your powerful vocal chords can paralyse a Mesophorkan, and even kill them should you scream.'

'I wish it would work on you,' Granny said.

'There are sentient vegetable life forms which fear humans' ability to chew them with those teeth – which are fearsome – 32 outcrops of bone, and powerful jaw muscles.

'The stories go around about how a human can carry on fighting for hours, even after you shoot it. You have a collection of bloody warrior gods like Rambo and Swarzenneger. What's more you can improvise weapons, and use them.

'And, you project bio-weapons from every orifice of your body. Travellers are advised that if they get into a fight with a human to always remove the head because a limb won't fatally incapacitate you.

'We learn that humans can detect you even at night by tracking vibrations through the air. And were you to start colonising other worlds, because you reproduce at the rate of one a year, many other life forms would grub out infestations immediately.

'But what makes you most feared is your endurance. There is evidence that your primitive ancestors would hunt a prey simply by following it at walking pace, without sleep or rest, until the quarry died of exhaustion.

'Your shock resistance and the ability to recover from injury is absurdly high. You don't need to be stronger than your prey, you simply outlast them. As your war leader Churchill said: "War is not about who is right, it is about who is left."

'Think about it. You practised surgery on each other

before you had anaesthetics. In extremes, you have even been know to perform surgery on yourselves and survive. You reinforce damaged body parts with metal.

And by god you will eat anything. You even season your food with borderline toxic spices.

'Just look what you do for fun. You jump out of a plane with just a flimsy pieces of cloth to stop you making a meat pancake.

'It's one thing to be hunted. You run away. But when your hunter keeps showing up day after day after day, tracking you by what you've left behind, fur, feather, footprints, urine, faeces... You wake and he's there again waiting – until you just die. Humans are scary.'

For once Granny was silent. They all were. Perhaps they were even thinking, "Can we use this"?

It was decision time. I turned back their clocks and tweaked their neural tissue with an extended hyper-affection for Emmerdale. 'Bugger them,' I thought. They had it coming.

· · · · ·

Cramer House

The drive had been covered in asphalt. It was out of character but I could understand the reasoning.

Cramer House had belonged to some minor aristocracy and now was home to an assortment of our aged. Stone steps stumbled to a portico with Palladian airs. In an effort to breathe brightness into the grimy stonework, the door had been painted at various times in primary colours, all of which were visible beneath the chipped surface. The colour scheme failed at every level.

I pressed the doorbell and was greeted by a rasping electric bleat too brash to be ignored. Behind me lay the rolling Shropshire countryside pregnant with late summer showers and I longed to return to it.

The doors parted, doors tall enough to accommodate any normal giant, revealing a diminutive doe-eyed young woman wearing a tabard over a stretched uniform. I was admitted and directed down the hall to the Regency room where residents were assembling for elevenses.

The giant door on a spring return pulled itself forcefully to behind me. A sickly warmth and the odour of past meals engulfed me. It was easy to identify the boiled fish. It was also difficult to ignore strident overtones of overcooked cabbage.

I moved down the hall and thought about knocking. I decided it wasn't necessary, adopted a cheery, it's-a-great-life smile, adjusted my day-to-day hypocrisy and pushed open the door. The room was large, bright and airy. The incumbents were collected in a selection of high-backed chairs stacked with improbable cushions.

One or two faces looked up and then returned to patience or some handicraft that had been foisted on them. The odour of warm urine now whetted my palette.

I found Mrs Brelisford whom I was visiting, and she found me a chair. It was still warm. We smiled at each other and exchanged small talk. I realised I had begun picking at something encrusted on the arm and immediately stopped.

Near the Adam fireplace a disturbance erupted among a group of residents. There was no fire, but they grouped around it probably from habit. One of the more vocal bellowed, 'Gwennie! Mrs Davies has had an accident. Gwennie!'

The word spread, not like wildfire, more like custard. Another resident leaned over conspiratorially and said to me: 'She's had an accident.' The word was taken up among the best of the rest. 'Bit of an accident.'

'What?'

'She's had a bit of an accident.'

And indeed she had, for the cloying smell of warm faeces began to fill the room as it must have just filled Mrs Davies' diaper.

Gwennie bustled in and bending towards Mrs Davies said, 'Had a bit of an accident, have we?'

I looked at my visitee. She nodded sagely. Gwennie released the brake on the hapless Mrs D's chariot and wheeled her smartly out of the room. An old codger in a far corner awoke to the smell and choked back, 'What's that bloody stink?'

I sensed I was about be enlisted into a fugue of

explanation when Mrs B said she had something to show me. She rose painfully from her seat and I was left looking for a way to avoid taking part in the excremental chorale that was being orchestrated with whispers and nudges.

I looked for something with which to be occupied. There was a magazine rack with Woman's World and incongruously Heat Magazine. I couldn't face either. They were warm and dog-eared like the residents and falling out of the rack just as the denizens of Cramer House were slipping out of their lives.

Mrs B. returned with a photograph of I know not whom. I could see it in her arthritic fingers as she zimmered back to me. I couldn't even pretend. I just said, 'Sorry – before my time.'

As the previous sweet stench melded with the afterburn of boiled milky coffee dispensed with fig roles and Garibaldi I made my excuses and left.

Outside near the car park a Rhododendron blossom held a few precious drops of rain. I gently shook them on my hand and splashed my face. It took several deep, deep breaths before I felt able to drive away. Some days are so fair. Some days are so blessed. Some days nobody dies at all.

• • • • •

68

Tormain Hospital

'Can I see him?'

'Of course Dr Graham. That's why you're here.'

'Where's he being held?'

'I'll take you. You won't have come across anything like this. He's on meds – not that it makes much difference. A reasoned and reasonable approach appears more affective than the seratonin trigger we implanted when he arrived. His manifestations weren't as extreme then.'

'I'm sorry Guy... I can call you Guy can't I? I've had to drop my case load; I have just driven across four counties... five, five counties to be here and I haven't given the case notes the time they deserve. In short, what exactly are we dealing with?'

'Have you read Professor Zante's paper, Current Expressions of Psychokinesis?'

'People moving objects with their mind?'

'And I'd prefer 'Dr Barlow' if you don't mind or Governor Barlow... Yes, moving objects and more. Sometimes creating illusions. Zante has documented 700 cases worldwide. And from that 700 we have Corin whom I'm sure you'll find fascinating.'

Suddenly Dr Barlow's well-appointed office trembled like an earthquake had struck. The walls bulged. A fissure opened in the side carrying the 'feature painting' and ran down behind the teak and chromium unit beneath. There was a hiatus. The painting swung precariously.

'Did you choose that?'

'Sorry?'

'The painting, was it your choice?'

'Yes, actually.'

'Very nice. What was that by the way?'

'That would be Corin getting restless. He's been expecting you for days.'

'You told him I was coming?'

'No, he just knows. He knows so much about all of us here we hardly give it a second thought – and frankly I don't think he does either. He's tired of showing off.'

'Right, let's go then.'

'If it looks like things are getting out of hand I'll pull you out.'

'Might not be a good...'

'The thing is, you may not know things are out of hand.'

The govenor rose from his desk and led the way. Dr Graham scurried to keep up. On route the sophisticated decor gave way to perfunctory white walls as they passed through security: guards, retinal scanners, keypads and voice codes.

They reached a gallery which overlooked eight cells. Most were empty.

On the far side behind tinted glass Dr Phil Graham could see several staff members bent over monitors.

'And they would be whom?'

'They are six of the 18 staff on rotation who look after the needs of Corin – doctors, nurses, technicians...'

'The rooms look like squash courts. They're not very homely are they.'

'That's why most of them are empty.'

'Right let's have a word with him. How do I get in?

Barlow nodded to the control room and a platform, big enough for one, traversed the length of the gallery and stopped above one of the occupied cells.

'Your lift, Dr Graham.'

Graham climbed aboard and gripped the handrail as he was lowered into the cell. The occupant didn't look at him but continued to stare from his seat at the metal rail at the foot of his bed.

Graham removed his overcoat and sat at the aluminium table. Corin turned to face him, and smiled warmly.

'Welcome to my, "umble 'ome", he said mimicking Graham's dialect.

Graham grimaced: 'I thought we might just get to know each other a bit as it seems I will be visiting you for a while.'

Corin took a seat opposite Dr Graham. His intense blue eyes fixed him.

'Well Phil... You don't mind if I call you Phil do you? You are harbouring doubts, scepticism – a little anxiety... Too little anxiety to be honest.

You are intrigued and mildly flattered that they have called you in to deal with – me.'

'Go on.'

'Let me short circuit this rigmarole. Look at the end of my bed.'

A flame appeared there glowing like a beacon. The room seemed to darken.

'That's very good Corin. May I...' He looked around distractedly, 'call you that? Got any more?'

'Oh so much. What did Marlowe say, "...and his

dominion that exceeds in this, stretcheth as far as doth the mind of man. A sound magician is a mighty god...".'

'Yes, something like that.'

'There was that summer's day, Dr Graham. Julie was wearing a pea-green cardigan. It shouldn't have suited her but you thought she looked magnificent. You are standing on the pier. It's been a beautiful day and the sun is kissing the afternoon goodbye with gold and magenta rays.'

'Very good again. So what is it you do, mind reading and illusions?'

'You must know something of physics, doctor. You are a 'doctor' after all. We have proved 11 dimensions but we only experience three; four if you count time. Two cars approach a crossroads...' He moved his hands slowly together. 'But they only collide if they arrive at the same moment – time.'

He clapped his palms forcefully together.

Graham's head spun as he fought his way back to reality from the passenger seat of a car about to be rammed.

'Once... you understand how your world... is brought to you by receptors... trying to interpret the data... you can see how flimsy... your knowledge... of everything outside your skull – really is.' Corin smiled benignly.

'But... That doesn't help you cope with normal life Corin...'

Graham was still struggling to recover from the illusion.

'Imagine,' Corin said, 'Someone in another dimension putting his fingers into our reality.' He whispered, 'How would it appear? Five large pink ovals floating in space?'

'Yes, I see but...'

'Your reality is open to me and I can give you any reality I choose.'

Graham found himself walking along a hedgerow at sunset. His dogs were bounding ahead. He felt a pressure in his ears. Turning, there was a barn owl following him low, looking for small prey. But he'd felt its presence not heard it.

A voice came over the intercom: 'Dr Graham, I think that's enough for today. Make your way to the lift.'

The blue eyes scrutinised his departure.

He was led outside the main gate and stood trying to place his car.

Inside Tormain Maximum Security Hospital Dr Graham was still sitting in the cell, staring at his hands and the play that was unfolding there; while outside... Outside Corin searched for the right car.

· · · · ·

The Last Tourist

Tristram watched the last three tourists board a plane and leave the island, then turned back to his monitor. It was hard to believe. The end of an era. The hotels had nearly all been re-assigned as office space or accommodation for the hi-tech brains flooding into the country – catching the wave of evolution – the new tourist-free landscape in which even repat' Cypriots no longer could demand a place as of right.

Now there seemed there were as many Asians and Eastern Bloc boffins as locals. Cyprus had fallen off the skewer of pitta politics and landed at the head of the table. The chain of events that changed its role was part accident and part coincidence.

In the mid-21st century some countries had tried to put a strangle hold on the world by controlling water. It was meant to be a trade off with the Arab States which still called the shots over oil.

Hardly anyone fell for it. The process of desalination had become cheaper and more efficient. Why would anyone buy it – unless they lived in the middle of a desert.

Cyprus had an abundance of free Mediterranean water, and all the solar power it needed. It was only when the South American Rainforest Association decided it needed to sell air that Cyprus became worried.

It was globally agreed that countries should pay densely-forested regions an amount inversely proportional to the forests on their own lands and directly proportional to their population – the forests being in effect the lungs of the planet. It was successfully argued at the World High Council that maintaining the forests was providing a resource without which the planet would die.

Here Cyprus saw a problem. It was not that 'big' on forests and 85 per cent of its population lived outside the country. In the future it was likely to be held to ransom by almost everyone, except the Arabs who still had the oil to bail them out.

What to do..? Well someone noticed that there was something quite important on Cyprus. Something that would make the world take notice if it could just grasp the opportunity.

Conceived during the Regan administration and brought to fruition under George Bush Jnr II, Son of Star Wars, missile platforms circling the Earth, could be aligned to spy on, or destroy any target on the planet. They could be directed to send a pinpoint laser beam, or a full nuclear strike, just about anywhere.

The snag, although it was spun as a safeguard, was that in order to work, tracking stations had to be placed outside the US. It was said that the allies of America therefore had a hand in determining the use or abuse of this frightening 'weapon of peace'. One would be in Yorkshire.

The galactically arrogant thing almost everyone overlooked was that one station, under British control, was on a base at Ay' Nic', Three Mile Point, Cyprus.

Neither the Chinese, the Russians, the Indians or the Pakistanis liked the idea of America looking over their garden walls and were keen to offer, albeit clandestinely, something in the way of expert advice should the Cypriots ever decide to do anything about it.

The Cypriots were at first amused and flattered. Then a group of army officers discussing in an informal way how they might defend areas around the Green Line, concluded that with a modest amount of force on a humid afternoon one could walk into the base almost by default.

In the past, retaliation was a fair reason for not attempting this, but with the expertise on offer, the tracking systems could quickly be brought under Cypriot control and the parent administrator locked out.

All this was possible because a valuable piece of Indian software on offer didn't crack the password codes or fail-safe devices – it simply dumped them and re-installed its own. It then embedded a safe set so the ploy could not be re-used.

The Russians provided guidance and control expertise and the Arabs provided lots and lots of money. So one August day Cyprus took control of 25 per cent of Son of Star Wars and began by cutting a hole in the deck of an American carrier.

When the US threats came, its missiles were aimed at Moscow who demanded America back down. The Russians still had enough of an arsenal to make the USA take notice. Every time a threat was perceived, Cyprus simply revolved the space platform and targeted the miscreant.

Eventually it was accepted as a fait accompli. And so Cyprus now controlled not just a weapon but to some extent the course of world events. Cyprus didn't seem particularly hostile. It demonstrated no grand designs on world domination. However when small requests were made for 'air', finance or expertise, countries fell over themselves to be amenable.

The best computer brains came to Cyprus and were

welcomed. It was a haven for science, and tourists became an inconvenience and a niggle to security.

So, 30 years on and the last three tourists were mounting the steps of an Airbus 980.

Tristram casually fed in some data.

'Running a small test,' he called across to his supervisor.

'No surprises,' the supervisor shouted back. 'I don't want any incidents.'

'Just my miserable brother-in-law; the bastard,' Trist' muttered under his breath. 'If he thinks he can jerk me around...'

The platform swung silently in space and a beam of laser light bored down burning a four-inch hole in the roof of a new white Mercedes parked somewhere in Hendon. A packet of pittas which lay on the back seat was completely incinerated but the halloumi nearby was cooked almost to perfection.

• • • • •

The Swirling Mist

The mist swirled before my eyes and began to clear. The headlines told me that somewhere in my universe it was daytime. Then the fog closed in again. It was as bad as a late November afternoon on the Staten Island Ferry.

I was washed back to consciousness. The fog began to lift. Sure I'd felt worse but can't remember when? I barely remembered my own name. There was a good reason for this. I didn't feel like someone I would want to know.

Then I made my first mistake – moving. I tried leaving my head till last, a tactic I'd developed in my early barroom years. It stopped the painful stuff rolling to fresh conflict zones inside my skull. The attempt was futile. I was in some sauna in the bowels of spa hell and one of Old Nick's sidemen was throwing buckets of firewater on the coals. I had it all – the sweats, the mist, the feeling that I needed to take that icy plunge off the ferry – even if it damn near killed me.

I remembered a cup of coffee on the nightstand and groped optimistically in its direction – my second mistake. Cup and contents clattered across the floor. Later would be soon enough to deal with it.

Visibility improved enough to see the upturned cup. Just beyond there was a pair of women's shoes complete with shapely legs rising from two ungainly feet. Something made me believe that by rotating my eyes while leaving my head sunk in the pillow, I would get a better view. The legs disappeared up inside a satin shift.

I levered myself on one arm. There stood the slim figure of what could be my nemesis, arms folded, one hip thrust forward, a look of controlled scorn on her not undistinguished face.

'You look like hell,' she said. What a greeting.

'Could you... Would you mind...' I almost gave up, '... not talking so loud.' The words came out like slurry from MacGyver's meat packing company.

'Do what?'

I took another shot at reconnecting my speech centre. It was as hopeless as asking the switchboard operator for a line to Big Frank in Hoboken on New Years. I swallowed hard and hoped I wouldn't have to repeat the exercise. 'Lady! Keep your voice down – please.' The connection was lost and my appeal sank into the pile of other garbage I may have also uttered during the last eight hours.

'Sugar, pass me my pants.'

She stared at me like a street kid looking at his first dead cat. 'Get 'em yourself.'

I looked around the floor for my cleanest shorts. Then I remembered. I was wearing them.

'Coming out,' I moaned,' and untangled myself from the bedcover, swung my legs out and launched myself toward the bathroom. I hoped to take my body by surprise before it realised I was seriously compromising its safety. There was a lurch in my reality as I reached the bathroom door, rather like a bad splice going through the projector at the local flea pit.

For a second nobody, including the projectionist, knows what is going to happen. In my case Old Nick was back with his band of sauna demons and I was getting loofahed inside my head.

I made it to the cold tap, filled the basin and pushed my head under the icy torrent. Old Nick disappeared as my consciousness took a hike over Niagra Falls in a leaky barrel.

'Who are you anyway?' I looked up at her. She picked up my pants from the floor and threw them at me. Right after she threw my gun and bill fold. I dropped the pants and caught the other two by reflex. The .38 was empty but the bill fold was loaded. Had it been the other way round it could have been dangerous. The safety was off.

'Who are you?' I repeated.

'I'm your damn cleaner,' she replied.

Dragging on my pants, for the first time I stood fully upright. 'How come you are undressed? Did we..?' She switched hips. 'Are you kidding? I got a husband and a kid.'

For a moment I was sorry – sorry we hadn't fallen into the sack together – lost ourselves in a few stolen hours. She was easy on the eye; probably mixed race; possibly Puerto Rican, but it was a plus. Her eyes were circled with regret and disappointment, and she carried herself with that world weariness you inherit when your last dream goes down the pan and you realise that nothing in your life will ever be better than it was last week.

'How come you're undressed?' I asked again.

'You're never here so I take off my dress while I work. You never see me 'cause you're never here.'

'What day is it?'

'It's Saturday. That's why you're never here. It's the day you eat breakfast, down at Mike's over on Third. I guess you didn't make it today.'

'No, guess I didn't – but I might still try.' A gallon of coffee, drug strength just might start my motor. I turned off the faucet and peered at the sad individual in the mirror, then at her. 'Say, do you think you might wanna' join me. Forget the cleaning today. Have breakfast... on me.'

She snorted. 'You sorry piece of crap. You think you're going to keep breakfast down. Anyone within 10 feet of you will be wiping your puke off his boots.'

She was probably right. Nevertheless I tried again. Experience had taught me that when in doubt you ask questions. 'Where's your husband?'

'He ain't here.'

'He ditched you?'

'Sonovabitch left me to bring up my boy alone. Bastard even picked the rent out my pocket book.'

Her words sank into some silent corner of the room.

'Have coffee with me,' I urged.

'I don't know you.'

'Yes you do. Sure you know me. It's Saturday morning and we both of us survived another lonely, miserable night. Let's pretend we're like two regular people and share a meal.'

She looked long and hard at me, then crossed the room to my dying Chesterfield. She lifted up her cotton, floral dress from the back of the sofa and slipped it over her head in one easy, fluid motion.

•••••

Would you convey my compliments to the purist who reads your proofs and tell him or her that I write in a sort of broken-down patois which is something like the way a Swiss waiter talks, and that when I split an infinitive, God damn it, I split it so it will stay split, and when I interrupt the velvety smoothness of my more or less literate syntax with a few sudden words of bar-room vernacular, that is done with the eyes wide open and the mind relaxed but attentive.

Raymond Chandler

Sam's Tale

Sam Needy spoke to me in bright circles. His prose sparkled in the air.

'Ah! The tales I can tell you,' he said. 'The stories, ripe with the hopefulness of new love; dark with discovery of one's own desire; hopeless in the tide of life's energy. Make peace with your past. It is only what you think you remember. Your future is imagination, an egg unpoached. Here and now is all you have.

'Where are you? Sitting alone – not being lonely, just alone? Is that you, now? Is that *your* now? Or are you sitting with friends, being friendly? Are you, conversing lightly, smiling, laughing, pushing your limits, just a little – for the laughs?

'Or have you descended into good works. Losing your pain in the pain of others. Giving up your life, offering your dedication, handing out full measure of self-sacrifice, not realising that in the end you will never... ...never have given enough.'

I should have listened. I could have listened more closely. Life had set me on a path. There was momentum. Sam on the other hand was the opposite. The force of inertia lay heavily with him. Newton's Second Law of Thermodynamics was expressing itself across time and into the bar room where we sat. He was one of Dublin's lost boys, fallen from grace, outplaced in England like some angel expelled.

And behind the wit, the humour, the readily turned phrase and the celestial acumen there was often a deep sadness. It frothed like the head of his beer around the rim of his existance in-self mockery and the occasional wry smile.

'You know what you should be doing,' he would say? 'You know what a young fella like yourself should be doing right now?'

And he would be right. He not only knew what was best for him, but what was best for you also. Sometimes I would see him in the corner of the bar with his pint before him, or standing by the back door with a fag burnt so low it was only good for lighting the next. I would go over with some idea of consoling him or listening to his woe. Before not too long it would be me coming away uplifted. I would have received some unsought unction mysteriously delivered.

Then, I remember the day quite well, I stepped into the saloon, and he'd gone. His place was empty. His lyricism on life and the town's inhabitants had been replaced by a television. Ironically a children's programme was being screened.

The pub's new owners seemed to like it. The old timers were trying to ignore it. Sam had simply left them to it.

'Where's old Sam,' I asked? 'Anyone seen him recently?'

The barman reached for the remote and switched over to 'Eggheads'. 'The old beggar's gone off, and good bloody riddance. Thank god the smell of him has gone. I don't think he changed that old brown suit in 30 years, hahaha!'

'What upset him then,' I asked?

'He took against the new telly. Said it was killing conversation. When he tried to shut it off I kicked his arse out of here on to the pavement.'

'You did what?'

'That's right. I put my big toe in his raggedy backside and hoisted him out.'

I felt an anger rise in me that I have felt on only one or two occasions in my life. Being a little wiser now, I reached in my pocket for my cheque book. I quietly made out a cheque for cash to the amount of £350 and handed it to the barman.

'What's this for,' he asked?

'This,' I said. And taking my pint pot, I drained the last half inch just before hurling the sturdy dimple mug through the poxy plasma screen.

Here and now is all you have.

· · · · ·

The Playground

It's odd how certain memories find daylight after years of neglect. Like some old photograph tucked behind the back of a drawer, they entice you to a flux in space and time. You re-emerge from that other place minutes later surprised and renewed by the re-acquaintance. But this particular recollection was more like a nail in my shoe; a nagging discomfort I'd learned to live with.

The fragrance of freshly-mown grass tugged at my senses, and became a scent memory of the school playing field. We, our little gang, were terrorizing younger boys by pushing them on to the heaps, and stuffing clippings down their shirts. Once we got deeper where the grass had begun to compost, we pelted them with gobby, gooey clumps.

It was early June and our little unit had already established itself. There was a pecking order certainly. Peter was at the top, there was no doubt about that. His blond good-looks and assured behaviour made him a natural. He also had the best dad. His dad could make models out of metal which really worked. Peter had a steam engine which he would occasionally exhibit. It was made clear that it was a particular honour to be at a viewing. We all envied Peter his dad, and would have done almost anything for a few moments in his exalted company.

Johno was Peter's accepted second in command. He lived across the avenue from Peter. They could plan our missions and training long after tea and we had returned home. Our little unit, our gang, although we didn't like that term, was constantly training for some event that

I was unable to imagine. We practised stealth; jumping from a high branch followed by a paratroop roll; spear throwing, and catapults. Sometimes we sneaked food and matches, and cooked bangers on long sticks in the coppice.

The fourth member, after me, was Bertie. He ran all the errands but didn't seem to mind so long as he was included. I was above Bertie and almost on a par with Johno.

As the young ones ran off mouthing empty threats about bigger brothers and dragging the grass out of their hair, we moved to the playground and began a game of tick. It was lively and we all showed good skills, darting and weaving away from the pursuer. Then I was on. I was the last of the four to be caught and I decided that my turn to chase the others would be short and swift.

I was wrong – so badly wrong. By now I was tiring. That day, to be on the safe side, mum had dressed me in warm apparel; heavy, grey, surge shorts, a brushed-cotton shirt and Fair Isle sleeveless pullover. It was a handicap. I was heating up at an alarming rate. I tried to tig the other members of our party but they were too quick, too nimble. At the last instant they would twist a shoulder away or contort their spines so that my fingers were within tantalising inches of the mark.

It became obvious that I was getting slower and hotter, giving them more recovery time. But then something else began to happen. Others could see the hapless quarry I had become and began to join the game. I had plenty of targets but couldn't tig one. The mass grew. It became a swarm that ebbed and flowed around my incompetent lunges; a wheeling, milling, rapacious cloud of starlings. Peter and Johno were urging the mob on, catcalling from the rear. Soon most of the playground had joined the swarm; a mad, raucous gang of children goading me and laughing at my helplessness. Then the taunting began and it grew. It grew into a chant that was taken up by all. I could see the faces of those I knew; children whom I thought were my friends.

They leered and jeered at me and I began to cry – hot, salty, stinging tears – tears of desperation and humiliation. There was just a small boy facing the whole playground alone – me – not having given up, but powerless before them all.

"La la, dee da da. La la, dee da da. La la, dee da da. La la, dee da da." And a whistle cut through the clamour. The swarm dispersed, melted away, and I was left looking up into the sympathetic but incredulous eyes of my teacher.

We moved inside. I was sat in the quiet corner while the rest of the class filed out for 'music and movement' in the hall. I raised my eyes from the embroidered handkerchief I had been given. Peter, Johno and Bertie were the last to leave. They came to attention and gave the salute we had practised, right arm outstretched at eye level. Peter and Johno's left arms were held down the seam of their pressed khaki shorts, their Airtex shirts crisp and the elastic belts with the snake clasps neatly in place.

Peter brushed the shock of blond hair from his forehead and surveyed me with snow-blue eyes. He smiled but the smile wasn't for me. Johno and he turned about and marched to the hall.

Bertie seemed divided in his loyalties but shrugged at me, gave a stupid grin and ran after them.

I always release the memory before it consumes me. I hate to go there but I'm still looking for some answer. You see, something happened that day – something important.

Mrs Norigi's Cat

They say you may choose your neighbours, but not your family. Probably true. We have little chance of escaping either.

Taking early retirement in the family home had felt right, but I hadn't counted on rubbing up against Mrs Norigi. God knows where she hailed from; some obscure Baltic, Slav/Russian extraction perhaps. I likened her to the Baba Yagar.

The Baba Yagar appears in Slavic folklore as a deformed or ferocious-looking woman who races around in a house mounted on chicken legs. And there she was, right next door to me.

We were slotted together in a compact Georgian terrace which wound steeply up a hill from the town centre. The houses though small at the front went back a good way, and had lengthy gardens.

Occasionally Mrs Norigi and I would exchange nods on the front step. Sometimes I heard her over the garden fence half chanting half singing strange ditties, or muttering obscure curses. At other times the sounds of crockery smashing or screeches broke through the wall.

What really offended me was the stink that oozed from there – old fish or boiled offal; and every so often the acrid tang of burnt feathers.

I cornered her one day. I said in my most inoffensive manner: 'Good heavens, what is that smell? They must be burning something... somewhere'.

'Cleenzing,' she replied cryptically and closed the door, rather too fast in fact because her sombre calf-length coat caught in the jam. After a frenzy of tugging the door reopened and she met my barely-concealed amusement with baleful glance.

I could always tell her comings and goings by her steel-tipped shoes which chattered up and down the street. Her calf-length dresses, navy or black, were always topped by a long drab coat, and a rag of a headscarf.

The smells sickened me as time went on. I peeked in her bin; then quickly forced down the lid. It held rotting fish, bits of intestines, and the remains of small animals.

About month five I understood. I saw her communing with a huge tabby cat. Its face, like a shrunken Bengal tiger, peeked from a skein of wild, knotted fur. She would pick it up, murmur, then point in the direction of my house. I deduced the stench must be Mrs Norigi cooking some banquet for the animal. It began eyeing me malevolently from the shrubbery opposite my bird table.

Visiting birds were a source of enjoyment. Over my Belfast sink with the wooden draining board which had served my parents for so many years, I watched them through the scullery window.

Throughout the summer the smells got worse. The cat and I went to war. The front line was the fence between Mrs Norigi and me. Whenever I caught it eyeing the birds, I dashed outside. It leapt up the fence with the speed of a Ferrari 350 GT, perched long enough to fix me with a death stare, then slid into Mrs Norigi's garden. Thereafter I would hear her banging a tin and calling, 'Vladim'.

My garden, the garden of my parents, was filled with shrubs, most of which I cannot name. They are a source of comfort. They bring me a feeling of continuity. At the far end are some fruit trees, apple and plum, but approaching the house are various sorts of shrubs and bedding plants.

Many began to wither and die. The cause was evident – Vladim.

One morning as I stepped out to restock the bird table I was upset to see my song thrush laid out stiffly on the step. From the garden Vladim's jaundiced gaze transfixed me. It turned, lifted its tale, and squatted over a delicate clump of pansies.

I grabbed a Wellington boot from behind the backdoor and hurled it at the animal. It spat then dived for cover. I saw Mrs Norigi watching from an upstairs window. All pretence of civility evaporated. If we met outside she would suck her teeth, curse under her breath then slip inside, ramming shut the door behind her.

Over the next couple of months Vlad' decimated the bird population. I complained but the tirade which exploded from the Baba Yagar's sallow cheeks would have made a sailor blush. 'You Inglich' she ridiculed, 'You are so soft'. 'Vladim he does vhat he does.'

For several weeks things quietened. I saw Mrs N' only a couple of times, once, oddly, walking backwards around her garden at night. Perhaps she was trying to cast the evil eye on me. I noted little strangenesses. Pieces of string with curious knots left on my doorstep; a piece of bone atop my Azalea. No coincidence there. It was plain the cat and Mrs Norigi were on the attack.

One day, as I entered the kitchen with a few apples from the garden, I found the chicken joint I'd left to thaw, on the floor with Vladim.

I quickly but quietly closed the back door. Vladim was braced for flight, except there was nowhere to run. I cautiously sat down to review the options. Vladim sensed he was not in immediate danger, and returned to licking the portion. Time slowed and the perfume of the lilies I had brought to cheer up the house filled my senses.

I drew one long stem from the vase and twiddled the flower head towards the cat. It shied at first, but then sensing it was involved in a game started clawing the flower. I teased him until in a frenzy he pounced and chewed. The pollen from the paprika-coloured stamens covered his chops. I repeated the game several times with more of the blooms. Vladim was suffused with success – chicken dinner, and he had out-manoeuvred several lilies.

What he couldn't sense is that the pollen of many types of lily is toxic to cats. I released him to the garden. It would only be a matter of time.

Two days later I heard the sound of a spade in earth. I am no stranger to the sound. I've served in extreme forward positions in Iraq, and Bosnia. I have battled for the rights of people like Mrs Norigi.

Even if she chooses to forsake her country for the relative peace of mine, I will not be spat upon in my own town by the very people whose freedom I have fought to preserve.

I went to my bedroom and looked into Mrs Norigi's garden. Sure enough she was digging a hole. I felt rather flat. I decided to treat myself to something; something I had been researching for a while, a new hi-fi system.

I stood surveying the adjoining wall of our houses and planned where I was going to hang the large, and extremely powerful monitor speakers. I was convinced they were going to make quite an impression on Mrs Norigi.

• • • • •

The World is Richer

The world is richer, vaster than it too often seems. Words can have colours and emotions. Numbers can have shapes and personalities.

You can be lured – sucked into the warmth of blanket soft, lullaby soft, serene, ghost touch. Like a May zephyr bringing hope of some warm idyll long promised.

There's a river. Listen to me. Listen to me. For a moment step back there. I kept your memories – safe. Nearly perfect. Almost new. Those you left behind when adulthood briar snagged the dew wet passion of your being.

Be practical. They said you should. And light limbed you stepped into grey rags that bent your shoulders as you joined the sad, halting road to here and now.

Around your neck no garland. In your hand no rose. No thorn to mark your flesh. No flecks of blood stealing sweetly down your pale skin. A bleak footpath to a city of tiny lights and empty promise.

Raise your arms about your breast. Please. Do it. Around your waist still fresh the wild flowers. Bee-sucked honey-loved essence nurtured in the mid-morning sunlight.

There was a time. Remember when there was no time at all. That cornflower moment you captured in its frailty and kept within the folds of this hooded graceless habit, stifled.

How many times have your searched within for that naked moment – for the dizzy laughter when you knew perfection? Then came confusion as it slipped away, giggling o'er the pebbles in the shallows.

Burbling into echoes, distant and past.

A different river now. Here on the bank slip from the robe and stand as you did once, free as you were once, impassioned by the mystery – enchanted by knowledge, rare strangely familiar, profound.

Lying in the live grass. Clouds like well-schooled orca migrate homeward to ancestral halls beyond our compass. Changes will come. Surely.

Late summer brings sadness at the squandered seconds. Yet there are still bright embers full brimmed with delight. To be engulfed... To be released with ravenous joy, desire unbridled... In that other world, that other life it is not wrong. It was the truth. There is no wrong. There is only truth and the acceptance of it.

Here at the boundary, overhung by rabid mounting foliage, there is no rational access. No broad trodden path back there. Ask around. No-one knows the way. Only when the siren sisters stir your inner voice do you slip beyond yourself at the threshold. How fearlessly you once plundered through to meet your wizened older nature.

Your avatar with considered measure calls the dance - slowly circling as you scent this long-lost hidden being.

We only see what we care about.

The exultation. The fearless joy. Dangerous, sexual.

And then late summer. There is the sad scent of wood smoke in the air. You look listlessly around. For a moment the world has slipped into neutral. Somewhere a dog is barking, a slow sonorous Morse-code bark punctuating the afternoon haze. Dash dash, dot; dash dash, dot.

What's to come? A leaf falls before your eyes from the great horse chestnut tree.

The dog has stopped and a woodpecker now raps the

afternoon silence, out of sight – somewhere.

You brace yourself for something yet to come. Some touch of change reminds you. Soon the bright mornings will be chilled. The sun moves carelessly south.

Sweet, poignant odour of dead leaves heralds new dark days. Along the road a stranger smuggles sunlight through the pitching trees. An old man walks in your imagination up Sandy Lane, and pauses to gaze at you through time. How can this be?

Our lives seem folded like coils, one generation against the next. And here I am gazing through the membrane, and he at me. It's permitted because we accept it is so.

Their laws are not ours. We have our knowing and our truth. I want you to look into me. Look and see how different I am. Know that the difference makes you free, for you are everything that is not me.

I have not spoken the words to you. Thoughtlessly I nearly said them out loud last night. They are eternal words and should not be said without conviction and strength. Sometimes they must be drawn from within like some spelk, some painful thorn. Sometimes they are forced out like a barbed hook that must go deeper before emerging between the painful tears. Sometime a whisper carries the message straight to the recipient's inner ear.

Bend close. I have something for you.

· · · · ·

War Games

It's difficult to say when it first started. Was it the Ludo? Was it Cluedo? What began as boyish games grew into a competitiveness barely matched by East v West in the cold war. The boys, Harry Featherstone and Billy Wildgoose, grew up on the same street in a Northern town.

Their quest for a new vehicle to challenge each other took them through, draughts, chess, dungeons and dragons and so on, until they finally locked horns in the arcane pursuit of war games. With a tidy sum invested in miniature soldiers, they recreated past conflicts and explored, 'What ifs'. And they kept tally of defeats, victories and dishonourable draws.

Both became fully paid up members of The Grufton Gamers and Historical Society in which they shared office, alternating between chairman and Hon' Sec'. As dedicated as they were, they failed to notice the dwindling numbers within their ranks until the two now aging gamers, were bearing most of the burden of hiring the Memorial Hall.

The hall had little to recommend it. It was a Victorian tribute to who knows what. You reached the main room via a stone staircase equipped with a no-frills iron handrail. The lavatories smelt of pine disinfectant, and the tea urn of warm gas. There was however room enough for the gamers to lay out tables of troops and space at the periphery for traders to offer miniature regiments from Sumeria to Stalingrad.

The rules of engagement were detailed and particular.

There were some historic portrayals of well-documented skirmishes, but the main action was in the centre of the hall. It was a knock out. The quarter finals came up. Harry and Bill were still in. The semi's happened and Harry and Bill were still there. It was no surprise to the remaining few of the few, that Billy Wildgoose was to face Harry Featherstone for the silver pot.

Everyone expected to see a fine display of gaming. Perhaps even innovative flexing of the rules. Harry won the first campaign. It was an approximation of the first war in recorded history. The armies met in Mesopotamia in 2,700 BC.

Billy bested his rival in round two. The Napoleonic battle, the Battle of Austerlitz, was one of the most important and decisive engagements of the Napoleonic Wars.

Napoleon gave every indication in the days before the engagement that his army was fragile, even abandoning the dominant Pratzen Heights near Austerlitz. However Billy already knew this, and was able to counter the bluff.

The tension between Harry and Bill was almost palpable. To their families they were a lost cause. The boyhood pals had turned into mean and bitter adversaries taking out petty hatreds vicariously through lead soldiers on a baize and papier maché landscape. They moved their pieces with considered malice and then stepped back to savour the effect.

The last exercise was from WW2. A few diehard members of the Grufton Gamers returned to watch this final conflict. Some interest had been stirred by Harry putting his fist right through the Pratzen Heights at the end of the second battle. The scent of a grudge match in a normally genteel pastime even attracted a reporter from the local rag hoping for a page five lead.

Under the Memorial Hall spotlights, play was set up for the finale, the Second Battle of El Alamein. It was the first major offensive in which the Allies achieved decisive victory against the Axis.

For Harry and Bill it was the culmination of 55 years struggle. This was it. This was the one in which the rancour of the decades would be exorcised.

Harry and Bill had read up on it for weeks and months. Billy thought the past was on his side. Monty would again lead the Desert Rats to victory. Harry was equally determined not to have history repeat itself. Rommel was acknowledged as a superb tactician by both sides.

Play began and continued through eight breaks, eight breaks.... The diehard fans were popping home for tea and returning later to see if the deadlock was broken. Outside an impending thunderstorm had raised the temperature up those stone stairs to an intolerable level. Spectators were dabbing brows with handkerchiefs and fanning themselves with programmes. Both competitors needed a change of shirt.

At 10.45pm an adjournment was proposed. Billy barked at the adjudicator and Harry rounded on Billy. A 10-minute slanging match then took place during which some spectators decided enough was enough and left.

It was agreed to continue – to midnight if necessary – when the room hire expired. Pieces started being placed quickly and resolutely. Asides, half-murmured insults, and derisive laughs marked the passage of play.

It looked like the battle was to follow the course of history, when Harry moved a tank to the front line. It was quite out of synch' with Rommel's tactics. Billy stopped in his tracks. Here was a sitting duck.

He crept around the table viewing the field of play from every angle, suspecting some unforeseen ploy. Finally he sank on his haunches at the end of the table, staring at the tank at eye level. It didn't look like the others. It was yellow – far too yellow. Not at all accurate.

And as he stared down at the mussel of the diminuitive Panzer, Harry leaned over and tapped the turret. There was a report – a puff of smoke – and from a small dark circle at the centre of Billy's forehead a ribbon of red began to make its way down his face. Spectators who were facing that direction reported seeing Billy's inquisitive gaze turn to incredulity just before he toppled sideways, his flailing arm bringing most of the battlefield with him.

Harry trod carefully through the toppled militaria, and looking down at his dead friend said simply: 'Bang, you're dead'.

The reporter took the stairs three at a time. As he hit the street the first large spots of rain began to wash the pavement.

● ● ● ● ●

Histoire Parisienne

I have a story for you, and like all good stories it is really a story within a story. It was recounted to me by a journalist friend at first hand.

To be plain I have been sitting on this tale for years. I didn't really feel it was mine to tell. However I think it is worth airing and now would seem to be as good a time as ever. I've changed the names, but to be honest I don't really remember some of them. Perhaps I never knew them.

The tale starts in France about 10 years ago. Franny, Samuel, and their daughter Sophia were holidaying in France somewhere south of Avignon. At some point they made the acquaintance of a young woman, Juliet, who needed assistance getting back to Paris. Her car had been stolen and in it all her belongings; suitcase, clothes, handbag, money and credit cards. She was distraught, desperate, vulnerable.

They quickly bundled her up and incorporated her into their travel arrangements. They gave her a lift, treated her to a few meals, and put her up in the pension in which they were staying overnight. On reaching the safety of Paris where she lived they hugged, waved goodbye, and then caught the Chunnel train back to UK.

Shortly afterwards a note arrived at their London home thanking them for the kindness shown to Juliet. It was signed by her father, Eric von Sternberg. The note asked that when next in Paris they should call at his home where it would be his pleasure to entertain them to dinner. Franny recognised the postcode as one of the more exclusive Paris neighbourhoods.

The Melnicks, Samuel and Franny were ardent Francophiles, and it wasn't too long before curiosity encouraged them to accept the invitation. Any excuse to re-aquaint themselves with la vie Parisienne was seized with enthusiasm. So it was only months later that they hauled up outside the imposing entrance to the Sternberg residence.

The house met all Franny's expectations. It sat in a tree-lined avenue. The taxi driver was unsure of the address and so dropped them several hundred yards away. When they found the gate it was a little rusty, the garden a tad neglected, strewn with the first fall of autumn leaves. The stone steps to the tall front door were worn but not dangerously so. The bellpush looked like a relic of another age but somewhere within the house they heard its muted ring.

Eric came to the door himself. He was lean, dark haired, wearing a grey cashmere sweater and old cords. His English had just a trace of an accent. They entered the vestibule and climbed the wide staircase past a collection of portraits to the study on the first floor. There they settled in comfortable button-back chairs and were plied with aperitifs and canapés – which they did not refuse. The room was reminiscent of a gentleman's club, elegant, and relaxing, steeped in the past.

Formalities were soon dispensed with; holiday events recounted, and the guests made warmly welcome. Clearly the generosity paid to Juliet by them was appreciated beyond the measure they anticipated.

At some point Eric left the room to check on dinner leaving Samuel, Franny, and daughter Sophia alone in the study. Sammy left his chair and began to stalk around the room examining the photos, pictures and curios. His attention was held by one particular photograph sitting on the large walnut desk. He was about to draw Fran's attention to it when Eric re-entered and conducted them to the dining room.

Eric, his daughter Juliet, Franny, Samuel and Sophia, took their places at a long, exquisitely decorated table, and were joined by an elderly aunt of the Sternbergs. The table setting incorporated elements of the traditional with a few contemporary touches. The guests feel privileged, but not intimidated.

The meal was of course delightful; the conversation flowed with the wine, and the company reached that wonderful stage during which a smile seems to pass around the room from person to person.

Fran became increasingly taken with the paintings along the dinning room walls. As the ageing aunt took early leave, and Eric disappeared to check on the pudding, Fran rose to examine the paintings more closely.

'Sammy, I think these paintings are real. I mean they are serious painters, Millet, Rousseau; that could be Cezanne, that might even be a Monet. Look! Look at the brushwork here. They must be worth a fortune.'

Samuel looked at her. 'Oh shit!'

'What?'

'Did you notice the photograph on Eric's desk?'

'Yes. Yes I did. The one of... Oh shit – you don't think...'

'Umhh!'

The picture that had caught Samuel's attention was of a high-ranking German officer, Teutonic bearing, silver hair, cropped short, an Iron Cross around his neck.

He was smiling across the decades at the now seriously perturbed Melnick family.

Eric returned to the table followed by the maid with the dessert course. He appeared unaware of the tension that had crept into the evening.

After several, thoughtful, spoonsful of a not unremarkable lemon and vanilla kugelhopf, Franny glanced across the table at her husband. He knew that look. She was going to go for it. Casually she remarked on the paintings; such treasures. How lucky to have such beautiful pieces in one's home.

It was something of an opening gambit. Eric agreed, and continued with his dessert. But Fran persisted. Was he a collector; had they been in his family long? Eric was not evasive but seemed disinclined to talk at length about the art work, except to admit that they were in fact genuine, and Fran had identified most of the artists correctly.

Finally he put down his fork, drew a linen serviette across his lips and looked thoughtfully at Fran with blue grey eyes that she thought concealed some slight amusement.

He pushed his plate to one side and said: 'The paintings – ah yes. I'm very lucky. They have been in my family a long time. I can see they hold your interest. But there's a rather interesting story connected to them. Would you like to hear it?'

They all said they would, so Eric suggested they return to the study for coffee and a perhaps a Cognac. When everyone was settled Eric began.

'I expect you have all noticed the photograph of my grandfather on the desk; another Eric as it happens. He was a remarkable man in so many ways. What you see in the picture is not completely representative of him. For instance, you might not have guessed, but he was actually one of the generals who plotted, and nearly succeeded, in assasinating Hitler. It was near the end of the war, and of course after that he had to hide out and wait for the inevitable. German High Command would have had him shot and so might the Allies.

'However, here I have to take you back a little further. During his military career he had taken some surprising, and often enlightened decisions. Significantly, at one point during the campaign he had come across a Polish Jew hiding in a railway station. The train was being loaded for the Death Camps. Mein Großvater didn't give the man away. Instead, he pushed him into an office cupboard, and ordered him to stay there until the train had left. Somehow he got him out of the station, pressed a roll of Deutschmarks on him, before directing him towards the American lines. It was an act that would have surely sealed his fate if he had been caught. In the end it was an act that saved him.

'At the time of the attempted coup on Hitler the allies were already pushing into Berlin. The city was being torn in two. The Russians were brutal, but no-one was being particularly nice. If you were military, particularly high ranking, you might face a firing squad or a noose. So grandfather threw away his general's uniform and took another from a dead corporal lying in a crater.

'Soon it was all over. Everywhere Germans soldiers were being mopped up and taken for questioning. Depending on your place of origin there were two lines. One went to the Russian side; the other to the Americans. Our family estate was in East Germany so Eric joined line of dejected, defeated humanity being summoned to account. Suddenly a hand grasped his arm.

"Don't stand in that line. You have no chance. Go in this one; the American one."

'He looked hard at his helper. For a moment he was totally bemused. Hunger and fatigue had dulled his senses. Then recognition dawned. Behind the warm dark brown eyes was the Polish Jew he had saved so many months before.

'He had made it to the American lines and had been co-opted as a translator.

'So, grandpa, Herr General von Sternberg, was sent through to the West annonymously with the help and support of his new Jewish sponsor. Later on he actually emigrated to the United States where he set up a successful garment factory, which in turn developed numerous ancilliary lines. In effect he remade the family fortune. But more than that.

'In the war all our possessions were lost. Our home, our land everything. Our estate, or what was our estate, was located in Soviet-controlled territory. Everything was gone, including the paintings you admired earlier.

'In time Eric sought out every painting he could, and bought them back at the going rate. It became his passion. And when he died my father continued the mission. So as you can guess I have an enormous fondness for these things. They represent far more than most people can imagine.'

The room fell silent. Sammy stared fixedly into his brandy sniffer. Fran touched away a little moisture at the corner of her eye, and Sophia found something of interest to study in the mouldings high in the corners of the room. Then the hiatus lifted and the warm smile they had all shared earlier seemed to circulate among them again.

After a little more small talk Samuel rose to his feet. 'I think we had better be going now. It has been a pleasure joining you for dinner and meeting you and your family.'

'And it has been a pleasure meeting you and your family Mr Melnick. I hope you will call and see us again next time you are in Paris.'

'I would like that very much Von Sternberg... Eric. I would like that very much indeed.'

•••••

112

Oh Yeh!

'Let me be frank,' she said.

'OK. You be Frank, I'll be Shirley.'

'Surely you can't be serious?'

'Sirius?'

'No – listen...'

Our situation hadn't improved in the last three hours – neither had our tempers despite the veneer of humour. You see, following advice I once read on being lost in Cyprus, I had followed a goat as it would I believed lead me to a village.

As we lost our footing and plunged into the small fissure, dragging the goat with us, I had one of those dazzling moments of clarity. It was a donkey; a donkey that leads you to a village not a goat. The goat always leads you to a cliff edge. I comforted myself that it was a simple enough mistake to make. Anyone could have made it.

Morning had passed. The sun was at its zenith somewhere. We were in the shadows, stuck in a cleft no more than a metre wide and barely enough room for the three of us. And we were in deep – too deep for anyone to reach the top, even if we stood on the goat.

He had choosen the central position – a fine Saarnan Bill'. I say "he" because we were up-close and personal. Crushed together as we were, I could fully experience his heady aroma.

Bill made early efforts to scale the wall but it proved impossible, even for him. My fiancée Judith, aka, "Frank", had borne the brunt of his effort. His sharp little hooves had raked my dearest's micro-fibre trousers bought for our walking holiday, shredding them, and causing a flesh wound which I suspected would likely become infected.

We lapsed into silence. Words were inappropriate. Finally Judith broke the impass.

'Come on honey,' she said. 'With your brains, your cunning and your athleticism you must be able to find a way out.'

'I'm trying,' I said.

'I wasn't talking to you,' she jeered.

Unperturbed by the slight I turned to Bill to see if he had anything useful to offer. He was wedged on his hind legs with his forelegs halfway up the rock. He turned to look at me with passionless yellow eyes. I held his inscrutable gaze – then decided a staring match with a goat was ridiculous.

At this point Bill made his contribution. He urinated, mostly over Judith. I wasn't too upset even by her colourful expletives. Only an hour earlier he had been trying to hump my leg so I felt it only fair the ignominy was shared.

Bill settled down to culling a little local flora. Then he closed his lidded eyes and seemed to settle in for the long wait.

This wasn't what I had wanted for the holiday. Our relationship, my relationship with Judith not Bill, had been suffering.

Well, the tonic prescribed was quality time together in a non-stressful situation. I had to laugh.

After another hour passed out of the blue Judith said, 'I've got this tune going round my head. I can't get rid of it.'

I searched for some trap, some hidden meaning, an ambush into which I was about to falter. 'What is it?'

'It's the Green Green Grass of Home,' she said. '"And then I wake and look around me, at four grey walls that surround me. And I realise – Yeh, I was only dreaming."'

I let her statement hang in the air. 'I know what you've got,' I replied.

'What's that?' she said thoughtfully.

Even Bill now seemed interested. With two quick snatches he tore a piece of fabric from the shoulder of my jacket, chewing with deliberation.

'You've got, Tom Jones syndrome.'

'Tom Jones syndrome?'

'Yes.'

She weighed my words. 'Is it common?'

'It's not unusual,' I said, delivering my line like a thrust of Toledo steel.

Couples often have a personal humour that shields them during times of stress. Ours failed here.

The goat came back for seconds of my jacket and nipped my flesh in the act.

'Sod off Bill,' I yelled.

'Oh, he has a name,' Judith snorted.

'There are 1,900 different sorts of plant on Cyprus and he is welcome to them all if he would just leave my jacket alone.' I gave him the hard stare. Bill turned to Judith expecting I know not what. In what seemed like a gesture of friendship he dipped his head towards her – then raked a horn up her ribs.

'That does it. That bloody does it. This is the last holiday I come on with you.'

Bill responded by crapping. It was an eloquent gesture on his part.

At that moment I heard rocks sliding and footsteps. Then there was a Cypriot voice followed by a face over the edge of our pit.

Hello mister. Hello lady. You found my goat – good. I throw down rope and you put it over his head. He looped a rope, and I passed it under Bill's chin and behind his horns. The farmer pulled hard. Bill took the strain and climbed... Well, he climbed like a goat.

Our new best friend reached down a strong arm for Judith. I followed on the end of the rope. As we dusted ourselves off, Stavros led Bill up to his dupla truck somewhere above the goat track.

Judith wouldn't meet my eye. 'I've lost the ring you bought me,' she said.

It was local silver, pretty but not expensive. 'It was a bit big. It slipped off. I think it may be back down there.' She nodded at the hole.

I peered over the edge. I could see it. It was sitting atop a pile of fresh goat dung.

'I'll get you another,' I said. But I never did.

Six months later we had divided up the books and CDs. She got the Sabatier kitchen knives and I got the Black and Decker drill.

She soon found someone else. He earned considerably more than me, so I guessed she would be happy. Me? I came back to Cyprus. Eventually I looked up Stavros and conversation eventually turned to Bill.

'He's dead,' he said.

I was stunned. How could it be?

'Bizarre laundry accident,' he said.

'What?'

'Bill, he was loner. He also very clumsy for a goat. He slipped.'

'What?'

'On the cliff behind Mrs Coufoudakis' house, he fell into her twin tub in the yard. It was quick, praise god, although...' He rubbed the back of his neck. '...Her spin-rinse cycle now... How you say...? Ferked?'

'Yes "ferked" would probably be it,' I concurred.

Instinctively I touched my shoulder – the tatoo mark from Bill's teeth still there....

Now, whenever I see a drove of goats scale a hillside, I wonder if Bill's kids might be among them. Wherever he is now I hope he has finally found the companions he truly deserves.

· · · · ·

The Snow Fox

There was the clatter of ski boots as one of the back-room tables got up to leave. Hans glanced from his beer briefly, and then continued conversation with the piste basher, the lift operator, the local policeman and another.

From the swirl of activity at the bar, Joseph the owner called to the three skiers zipping up their snow gear ready to meet the cold.

'Where you boys going? Hope you aren't going to try the pass. It's blocked. Bunk down upstairs and see what it looks like tomorrow morning.'

'No, we have to go. I have an early meeting. It'll be fine.'

Joseph peered into the back and found Hans a craggy old professional, in his usual seat chewing the fat with the other village patriarchs.

'Hans are you going down? Go with them.'

Hans peered through the fug at the three readying to leave. They were the current crop of hot young aces, all good skiers, but lacking experience; particularly night experience. Up here everyone spent four months of the year strapped to a pair of skis, but experience brought caution in a terrain as deadly as it is beautiful.

'It's OK,' Peter Grubber, the leader of the three, called back. 'We're good.'

At this point the police sergeant, Charles Matter, lifted his head. 'You go with Hans or not at all.'

'But...'

'If you want to keep your jobs at ski school you do as I say. That's it. Final.'

Hans looked questioningly at the policeman. He hadn't planned on the descent tonight.

Charles shrugged. 'Sorry Hans, but if they start racing in the dark someone will get hurt. They need guiding. You were going down tonight weren't you?'

Hans shrugged back. 'It seems so.'

'So Hans, how about it? We go?', Peter yelled.

'Yes, give me a minute.'

He made his "goodnights" and gathered up his pack. At the bar he picked up some chocolate and held it up for Joseph to add to the tab. Outside the three were already stepping into their bindings. They wore top-of-the-range gear, Gortex outers over hi-tech' merino. Hans wore a reindeer-skin cagoule, and old skiboard trousers. His boots harked back to his racing days when he was king of the slopes. He stooped and tightened them.

The three young men were full of themselves. He'd seen them come and go; brash, fearless – accidents waiting to happen. He adjusted the small knapsack, stretched in his bindings, and kicked off down the slope. The moon, big and full was behind them.

He didn't head straight down but peeled off to the side so he could check they were behind him. The night was startling in its brightness. The air was frost sharp and his breath a tell-tale life force.

The lads were whooping and caterwauling behind him. He needed to know how drunk they might be so he plunged straight down the slope to the blackness of the firs. They realised that the bar had been raised and the shouting stopped. The blackness of the forest would be a shock to them. You had to have your wits about you. Straddling a tree at 30mph was as painful as it was humiliating.

As they broke from trees Hans was breathing heavily from the forest slalom. There was now a fast downhill section on beaten piste. This is where he thought they would try to leave him behind.

For the young hot heads to lead old Hans down the hill to his own village would be the end of his legend. In with the new. Out with the old. He heard their skis carving the glittering lucent surface at his heels. They were pressing him.

His thighs complained as he leaned harder into the bindings. His skis were a little faster than their carvers, but harder to control. He was going to have to be at the top of his game. Peter was almost alongside him now. And already smiling the smile of the generous victor. But it wasn't over yet. A small mogul field lay ahead. Hans went to the left, hit a ramp, and cleared the field in one magnificent arc.

He had gained a little, but was tiring. The effort, the concentration... To hit rock or branch on this fast moonlight downhill could put one or all of them in the clinic. They were gaining confidence. Their laughter ran amid the sound of Kevlar and steel slicing packed snow. He decided to veer off piste to a steep powder-filled valley. The reflection of the moon on the vast white expanse was an experience he always savoured. He sat back a little to keep his ski tips out of the flume of frosty white clouds swelling around his track.

The three pursuants had fallen behind a little. They knew the bar had been raised once more. Hans broke right and headed for another section of trees. His knee was starting to trouble him now, the one he broke in the Regionals in '78. He began to go into himself for stamina. There were tricks. Sometimes you used the pain. Sometimes you used a distraction, or at a higher level you entered another zone where body seems to separate from mind.

They had negotiated the difficulties of the forest before he realised. Two of the party called to him that they were peeling off for their own village, a simple, short two-mile run down a blue slope. He raised a ski pole to them.

Peter shouted: 'Come on Hans. You and me. Race you.'

Hans kicked off again and headed down the Col. It was testing in daylight, but the young man at his heals clearly felt his equal. Hans re-entered the zone. All his experience was being pushed to the limit. He had the sensation he was flying and he had taken young Peter Grubber with him. They were both in some ethereal bubble high above it all, looking down on the village lights below. It was a gift from the mountain. He'd felt it before.

Suddenly he heard Peter's voice. 'Goodnight Hans; a great run. See you at the Hutte. Beer's on me I think.'

They were at the village outskirts. He could remember nothing of the last section. He lifted a pole to Peter. He had nearly got him, but not this night. Hans was still king of the valley.

'You know what you are Hans? You are an old fox – a snow fox.'

Hans stepped out of his bindings. He was at his house. He stood his skis in the porch and went inside to the warmth of a wood stove and the rich smell of home cooking.

His wife looked up. 'I didn't expect you tonight. Thought you would come down tomorrow, if they clear the pass. How did you come down?' Hans...?

As the moonlight flooded the window the snow fox smiled a smile.

• • • • •

Preston Gubbals has been Flattened

PICKERING: There's a problem.
CORSTON: (DISTRACTED) What..?
PICK: Preston Gubbals was flattened.
CORS: What?
PICK: Preston Gubbals...
CORS: I heard.
PICK: Oh! Then... You mean...
CORS: How?
PICK: Yes, 'how'. Well, that's not the problem.
CORS: (INTAKE) Oh, good.
PICK: They've invoked 'Sanctuary', so, it can't be flattened. It has to be restored.
CORS: Really? Can they do that – the Sanctuary thing?
PICK: Oh yes. There's a precedent. Westgate versus Goodwin, 2011.
CORS: I see. That's all going to take quite a bit of rearranging for someone.
PICK: (PAUSE) That would be me then.
CORS: Umh!
PICK: There's a rather awkward knock-on effect too. The Vada contingent has moved its HQ to Weston Lullingfields as its counter gambit, so we are having to consider recalibrating the parameters for the whole of the North West. I don't know how we will be able to cope. We don't have the resources.

CORS: You'd better put in a chitty ASAP. Get the wheels in motion.

PICK: Considering the number of chitties we have sent already the section head must be covered in chitty. They just don't seem to realise how thin the fabric of the illusion has become. I currently have one motorist on the Wrexham bypass who has been overtaken four times by the same rust-red pickup-truck with rear bumper hanging off.

CORS: The game can't last that much longer. The variations must nearly be played out; certainly within the next two or three hundred years. I'll have a word with Rodenhurst. See if we can't get something done about all this.

PICK: I'm on the verge of going back to 'Botanical'. Apart from autumn and spring everything just about takes care of itself. The conifers need no maintenance. The alpines are a dream. Even the tropicals are predictable.

CORS: You would be sadly missed Pickering. No-one has been able to cope with, 'people', as you do . No-one.

PICK: Well I for one will be delighted when this whole charade is wrapped up. To be honest I'm uncomfortable with the dishonesty. These poor beings playing out variations on a theme believing in free will. They have nothing with which to compare it. It's unfair.

CORS: There's bell ringing.

PICK: Excuse me?

CORS: Campanology I think they call it. You ring a 'method'. You start 1,2,3,4,5,6,7,8, keep changing the order and don't stop until it comes back around again to 1,2,3,4,5, etc. And there must be no repeats.

PICK: I really don't think any of the emerging prophets will take camp-whatsit-ology as his redeeming message to the masses.

CORS: You're probably right, as usual, Pickering. I know – let's create a diversion while we sort this out. How about dinosaur bones in Llyn Neeal.

PICK: It's pronounced Lynyul. Corston – for heaven's sake. But a fossil-find might hold their attention for long enough to put Preston Gubbals back.

CORS: Did you know it was mentioned in the Domesday Book? Emphasis on 'doom', eh? Some priest fellow with the Old English name of God's Bollocks or the like was a sub-tenant. (PAUSE) I don't know where they get them from.

PICK: Is that what you want in my report Corston? They flattened God's Bollocks but we made it all right with a Stegosaurus?

CORS: I think it will be a, D'ya-think-they-saurus, Pickering. Get it? Do-you-think-they-saw-us? (CHUCKLES)

• • • • •

Mad as Hell

'I am mad as hell and I and not going to take it any more.' It's odd the way lines from some films strike a chord. That one was delivered by that accomplished, and underrated English actor, Peter Finch, in a role as a TV newscaster suffering a nervous breakdown.

In the film, he more or less hijacks the network and shares his angst with the viewing audience. The ratings soar and of course he is encouraged to sound off nightly. In the process he encourages the public to, 'Get mad; stick their heads out of the window and yell the phrase into the city night...' And thousands do. Well I am mad as hell, and it's all about being processed by airports, aircrew and civil aviation in general. I am mad as hell and I am not going to take it any more.

Haven't you ever wondered why when you enter an airport you have to hand over all responsibility for your life? The moment you walk through those doors they do what they like to you.

Delays seem to be increasing. They take your luggage and then tell you how long the delay will be this time. Never mind that you are checking in at least two hours before departure presumably for their convenience. To be told that you must sit around for and extra five hours would try the patience of a saint, and the pocket of a merchant banker – except that he and all the other exec's are sitting in a comfortable business-class lounge with free drinks and all the extras which we, their customers, are unwittingly funding.

Yes, the international airport is a strange, confusing

place – at least for the first 90 minutes. It has its own global life – places to eat, places to buy clothes in case the delay is more than two months, sports shops in case you forgot to pack your pitons or mountain bike, and the compulsory display of naff ties, tartan covered dolls in cryogenic packaging and indestructible Kendal Mint Cake. You see, you are being encouraged in a galactically stupid way to believe your holiday, if in fact you are on holiday, has begun the moment you entered the airport Twilight Zone.

Airports make vast mounts of revenue, thousands of pounds for every 10 minutes a flight is delayed. There is no power on Earth which would force them to fly on time in the face of lucre accrued by the hold-up. Trains can't leave when they want to – well perhaps that's not such a great example...

In fact, now I come to think of it, it is difficult to recall anything that happens when it is supposed to; but at least you are free to leave the railway station and go to the pub or home or anywhere else for that matter.

It might not be quite so intolerable if you were made comfortable. Airport seating is designed to keep you circulating from Tie Rack to Duty Free, and on to the eatery decorated with something like plastic replicas of the leftovers from the rebuild of a Sopwith Camel.

And talking of Sopwith Camels – why are there never any spare planes to cope with the delays? My memories of the steam era and the Great Western Railway remind me that they could at a pinch always hook up the Gobowen Flyer, a 2-4-0 tank engine, to haul stranded passengers on to their destination or even one of the worthy Castle-class engines.

There are strong arguments for bringing an old Comet

out of the hanger (but not the lethal model with the square windows) with couchette and full silver service.

It used to be exciting stepping on to the asphalt and striding, bag in hand towards the great, silver aircraft. You felt like someone important – in a movie. We now seem to board like rats down a drainpipe, strap ourselves in ludicrously small seats and wait hopefully for the food parcels to arrive.

And don't be fooled if the airline offers you a menu. By time they hand out your package you will have only one choice. It will include either sweetcorn, reconstituted egg omelette, something brown in gravy and a brightly coloured thing with Miracle Whip piped on top, or possibly all of the latter.

You will of course be supplied with plastic cutlery so you cannot attempt to disembowel yourself when reruns of Only Fools and Horses, One Foot in the Grave, or worse, The Best of Terry and June are flashed on the screen before you.

You may of course sleep but this is only due to oxygen starvation when the air conditioning is turned down to save more money.

You know that no matter what time you started, no matter how long the flight is, no matter that your hotel is within a Sunday afternoon stroll of the airport, it is going to take a full day of your life and all your endurance to reach your destination.

You might as well sit back and enjoy the second bout of security questioning cunningly designed to trap you into confessing, "Yes, I am an international terrorist and my reason for visiting is to start a revolution and take control of the state." And, "I had a dark, swarthy stranger with a foreign accent pack my suitcase with the heavy metal sphere. The bottles with the skull and crossbones are for my personal use in case the flight is delayed and the only electrical goods I have are my Yamaha Melotone organ and some specialised detonating equipment which I need for my work. The Samurai sword is, of course, our picnic knife and I never go anywhere without it. I am of course much younger in the passport photo owing to the flight delays incurred on route."

There is, however, one thing worse than being an international terrorist, and that is being a smoker. My partner smokes and in sympathy I have an occasional cigar – well actually I am up to one a day now.

I read that the chances of contracting a serious illness from passive smoking is 30,000 to one. You might think those odds a little high until you comprehend that you are more likely to contract cancer from eating a carrot a day, eating a pork chop a week, drinking a glass of orange juice a fortnight or eating a head of lettuce every two years than, 'Sitting routinely in a roomful of smokers.' In fact the writer says that you are five times more likely to contract cancer from your budgie than from secondary smoke. Please address any queries on diet or pets to Mr Bill Bryson, New Hampshire, USA.

The galling thing is that after being dehumanised by the airport machine, smokers are asked to declare themselves subhuman, place themselves in booths and designated areas and generally conduct themselves in a way reminiscent of pinning on a yellow star in wartime Germany.

Where will it end? Shouldn't people with offensive body odour be cordoned off or made to travel in the hold; tiny children medicated so that they do not disturb passengers who have paid full fares and the people who contrived this whole travel nightmare forced to be available, and accountable, when we tell them, "We are mad as hell, and we are not going to take it any more"?

• • • • •

Flight of Fancy

SCENE 1

A BAKER'S SHOP IN A MARKET TOWN. JOYCE IS AT THE COUNTER BEING SERVED BY DOREEN.

F/X: SHOP DOOR OPENS AND BELL RINGS. MRS CRUFTINS ENTERS

JOYCE: Oh hello Mrs Cruftins. How've you been keeping?

CRUFTINS: Hello Joyce – not so bad.

F/X: DOOR CLOSES

JOYCE: And your Bill?

CRUFTINS: Oh, it's that Leibnitz again. It's really upset him. I fancy a few of those drop scones. I thought the Wittgenstein was bad enough but Leibnitz has given him a right turn. Put me up a dozen of the drop scones dear; and a quarter of the ham; the breaded...

JOYCE: I'm not surprised Mrs C. What's Leibnitz done for anyone? Bad as Hegel if you ask me. I like the look of those Danish. But I'm going to be very bad and have cream horn.

CRUFTINS: What about your Antony, Joyce?

JOYCE: Oh he's had his tribulations too. Mostly over the Wright Brothers.

CRUFTINS: Oh, they're not still pedalling that old chestnut, surely, Joyce?

JOYCE: Yes, and Antony won't put up with it any longer. He almost went ballistic.

CRUFTINS: Don't tell me – Clément Ader, 1890, beat the Wright Brothers by what... thirteen years?

JOYCE: That's right. The whole contraption only weighed 300 kg, if I remember rightly. It was October 9, 1890, he made the attempt. He flew approximately 50 yards (BEAT) if you can believe the French. (BEAT) He could've walked it.

CRUFTINS: I do know what you mean. The French like everyone to think they are responsible for croissants too when it was the perishing Austrians. (BEAT) Put me up two croissants dear while you're there.

JOYCE: (LOW) The experts say his work on the second aircraft was never completed. However Ader said that he flew the Avion II in August 1892 for a distance of 200m. (PAUSE) But that's not the problem.

CRUFTINS: Oh the 'experts'... They think they know it all. If it wasn't Ader then a pound to a penny it must be that Cornish New Zealander – what was his name?

DOREEN: Would you like the plain croissants Mrs Cruftins or we have some very nice pain au chocolat, fresh this morning? It was Pearse wasn't it, 1903 – a full nine months before the Wrights and their little Kittyhawk extravaganza?

CRUFTINS: Just the ordinary Doreen luv. Did you know they call them chocolatine in South-West France, (PAUSE) and in French Canada. Bill likes to dunk them in his 'confiture du fraise des bois' before a quick swirl in his bowl of café au lait.

JOYCE: He always was a man of refined tastes, your Bill.

CRUFTINS: No more than your Antony, Joyce. Doreen's right though – about Pearse... I still think the documentary evidence to support his claim remains open to interpretation. (PAUSE) No, the one I'm thinking of was that Lord.

DOREEN: Can I get anyone anything else?

CRUFTINS: I'm still deciding, Doreen luv. Serve someone else first.

JOYCE: Oh him. I'm not sure he was a Lord? He was definitely a 'Sir' though. Cayely – that was his name. Very clever man. Very clever... Very clever indeed.

CRUFTINS: The Americans (BEAT) They think they can do it all, but they can't. They can't do cheese... That reminds me... Doreen luv have you got any of that nice fatty Lancs?

DOREEN: Sorry, it's only the 'three-day Lancs' this week they didn't deliver the fatty.

CRUFTINS: Cut me six ounces will you? Not from that side luv; the other... Take it from the other.

JOYCE: It makes you wonder what Orville and Wilbur might have achieved if they hadn't had such an impoverished diet. Who can survive on Monterey Jack, I ask you?

DOREEN: Sir George Cayley is a distant relation of mine.

CRUFTINS: Never mind about that Doreen luv.

JOYCE: You see, in between being MP for Scarborough, he helped found the Royal Polytechnic Institution...

DOREEN: It's now the University of Westminster...

JOYCE: ...and was a founding member of the

British Association for the Advancement of Science.

CRUFTINS: I know. Putting aside all his work on: lifeboats; tension-spoke wheels; caterpillar tractors; automatic signals for railway crossings; seat belts, small scale helicopters, and a kind of prototypical internal combustion engine fuelled by gunpowder. He also contributed in the fields of prosthetics, air engines, electricity, theatre architecture, ballistics, optics and land reclamation.

CRUFTINS: So, what is it? What's got Antony so distressed

JOYCE: (LOW) It's the actual journey.

CRUFTINS: (LOW) Really.

JOYCE: In 1853, across the shelving meadowland of Brompton Dale, near Scarborough, from the high east side to the west, Sir George launched a machine that embodied all the basic features of what was to become the aeroplane; (BEAT) as we all know. It is rightly regarded as the first man-carrying flight by a heavier-than-air machine – the true birth of the aeroplane. (PAUSE) But Sir George wasn't in it.

CRUFTINS: You don't say. Who was then?

JOYCE: It was Cayley's coachman. And on landing he shouted: "Please Sir George, I wish to give notice. I was hired to drive, not fly."

DOREEN: Did you know that at some point prior to 1849 Cayley; my relation; designed and built a triplane powered with 'flappers' in which an unknown 10-year-old boy flew. Later, with the assistance of his grandson, George John Cayley, and his resident engineer, Thomas Vick, he developed a larger scale glider, also probably fitted with 'flappers', which flew across Brompton Dale in 1853.

CRUFTINS: Yes, thank you Doreen. Have you got any haslet this week? The last lot was curling at the edges. I had to put the dried bits in the centre of Bill's sandwiches so he wouldn't notice.

DORREN: Is a quarter alright?

CRUFTINS: Lovely Doreen. (BEAT) I think I'd better get going now or I'll never catch up.

JOYCE: Cheerio! Are you off home now?

CRUFTINS: In a bit. I have to call in on young Mickey Brewster's boy. He needs help with his thesis. He's trying to convince his tutor he knows something about the Chemistry of Porphyrins and Related Compounds.

DOREEN: He should look at the work of Professor Lionel Milgrom at Imperial.

CRUFTINS: Yes, thank you Doreen luv. (PAUSE) How much does all that come to?

DOREEN`: Ten and six please.

CRUFTINS: Take care now Joyce. Remember me to Antony won't you. (PAUSE) Doreen luv. Don't get me wrong but I think you should just concentrate on your cakes (BEAT) if you don't mind my saying.

F/X: SHOP DOOR BELL RINGS, DOOR CLOSES

•••••

I never thought it would come to this

'Then he said, "I never thought it would come to this".'
'Meaning what?'
'I've no idea.'
'But really...'
'No really, I've really no idea.'
'Well he must have meant something?'
'Yes, I suppose so but, when I saw him he gave me no indication of what that meant.'
'How long were you with him?'
'No more than a few minutes. He didn't want to talk to anyone from the office.'
'Why ever not?'
'He seems scared that someone – someone in this department was out to get him. He inferred that much. He feels safer inside.'
'So that's what the trail of petty crimes was about.'
'Yes, apparently... ...ending in his gross insults towards the judge.'
'Just let me walk through this again. He began by calling the traffic warden a neo Nazi, neo fascist, jackbooted, holocaust revivalist, power-mad, Wagner-loving, Alsatian faced, megalomaniacal, sauerkraut eating, sausage jockey with a penchant for mass murder and generally pissing off everyone around. He then assaulted the policeman called as back up.
'Yes, quite spectacularly.'
'Did he indeed?'

'He debagged the officer.'

'Debagged him?'

'Yes he did – completely.'

'So his training in unarmed combat wasn't entirely wasted one might say.'

'But this was just a precursor in his plan.'

'To get to the judge?'

'Precisely. He was held overnight in the cells and when brought before the Muppets...'

'Muppets?'

Yes, sorry, the local magistrates. He convinced them in less than a minute to refer him to a Crown Court where he could be dealt with in a manner reflecting his attitude to Her Majesty's Law Enforcement Officers.'

'And he continued in a similar manner with the judge?'

'Yes he did. He remarked on Justice Overleigh's pantomime costume and predilection for S and M in the shadier quarters of Soho, Wednesday nights.'

'No truth in that I suppose?'

'Well I actually believe he might have been on to something there. Would you like me to check?'

'Not now.'

'Judge Overleigh sent him down to reconsider is ill-chosen insults, and to prepare a proper apology befitting the gross nature of his words. His sentence would then be considered.'

'Well tell the fool to say sorry and let's get him out. We are short staffed with operatives as it is. There is that trade delegation coming in from the Ukraine and we can't have them wandering all over Whitehall without nursemaids.'

'This is the difficult part...'

'What?'

'It is his right to stay in prison as long as he likes. Until he apologises to the judge he can remain inside indefinitely. It is one of those legal quirks in our system.'

'You mean they can't get him out of there? We can't get him out of there?'

'That's about the size of it, I'm afraid.'

'OK then. We must look into his concerns, and have him genuflect before the Bench before the start of the final test at The Oval. I don't want to be standing in Brixton with an ounce of Old Holborne in my hand waiting for the silly bugger to come out from under his rock. Not when I could be enjoying one of Mr Minty's ham salad rolls and a cool glass of something alcoholic while the eternal struggle is played out beneath the gas works. I refer to the cricket and not my digestive system.'

'You put is so well sir.'

'I thought so.'

'There is just one thing. I'm worried he may continue his shenanigans into solitary to maintain the protection he believes the prison system can offer, and that we can not.

'Where was he before all this started?'

'He was living rough in Hammersmith.'

'Good Lord!'

'Undercover.'

'Really! Well I suppose it's better than working the late shift at...'

'At...?'

'Never mind. You'll just have to go and talk him out.'

'How sir?'

'Get yourself arrested same as him.'

'But...'

'Obviously we can't be seen to have any interest in him in his role as unfortunate vagrant – if that is what his cover is. As a secret Government agency of high standing – we are still secret aren't we? – there is no way for any of us to formally approach the prison for special visiting rights. And we can't ask anyone else to do it for us, for much the same reason.

You simply have to get yourself banged up in chokey and sort out the problem from there.'

'How do you suggest I go about that?'

'Well you could insult a judge. That seems to work pretty well. And don't apologise until you've got our man back in the fold.'

'Dear me. I never thought it would come to this.'

'Funny, that's exactly what he said.'

• • • • •

In the Beginning was the Word

In the beginning was the Word, and the Word was with God, and the Word was God. The word was, 'Bang'; big bang; bing banga bing bang. The first almighty sound in existence. And we still hear the echoes throughout the universe, carried across time; echoes that are vibrations. And before 'before,' there was no time – time did not exist.

Vibrations are energy. Some we perceive as sound; some as light. Some act as the binding force that keeps an atom together for example hydrogen which constitutes 90 per cent of the visible universe.

Humans are: 99 per cent hydrogen, one proton, one electron; oxygen, eight electrons, eight protons, eight neutrons; carbon, six protons, six neutrons, six electrons; all mysteriously vibrating away; sound that is not recognised as sound.

Interestingly a large number of atoms – about seven with 27 zeros of them – sometimes conspire to make a human, for 70, 80, 90, 100 years or more, until one day suddenly they do not. They stop co-operating. They go back to, or on from, what they did before taking on the interesting combinations that are us.

These vibrating particles of joy sing our uniqueness through the solar system. In a sense everything tangible, and a great deal that is not, is also resonating with, and against one another.

Pythagoras is attributed with first identifying that the pitch of a musical note is in proportion to the length of the string that produces it, and also that intervals between harmonious sound frequencies form simple numerical ratios. In a theory known as the Harmony of the Spheres, Pythagoras proposed that the Sun, Moon and planets all emit their own unique hum or orbital resonance based on their orbital revolution. He suggested that the quality of life on Earth reflects the tenor of celestial sounds which are imperceptible to the human ear.

Subsequently, Plato described astronomy and music as "twinned" studies of sensual recognition – astronomy for the eyes, and music for the ears.

Both require knowledge of numerical proportions.

Subliminally we are all aware of our link with sound. Ancient sacred places enhanced it in their construction. Lofty cathedrals also enjoy the uplifting reverberations of choir and organ. And tribal music has survived; survived from our ancestors' campfires, and becomes alive and well in the EDM scene enjoyed by thousands each and every weekend.

Technology now has produced speakers which allow sub bass notes to be physically felt. Producers are making music impossible a mere 40 or 50 years ago, simply because there wasn't the equipment available to reproduce it.

In a throng where the music, the vibration is everything, the urge to dance becomes inescapable – no longer as a courtship ritual, but as a celebration and affirmation of our place in this universe. This is the truth rediscovered by this generation – we belong here, and we belong to each other.

As John Donne said: 'Every man is a piece of the continent, a part of the main.

"... And therefore never send to know for whom the bell tolls..." It tolls... and tolls... tolls... and tolls...

• • • • •

Café Crême

He recognised Ira immediately. Actually he 'identified' her. It was their first meeting. He had arrived early, but she had arrived even earlier. It wasn't hard to pick her out. She was the only black woman in the café. In some ways the Turnbull Tea Rooms was a curious choice. It was a quintessential English institution. He anticipated she'd go for a soul food bar or something outré.

She half rose and gave a shy little wave. He waved back. From her point of view Robert looked even better than expected. Perhaps this wouldn't be the trial she'd feared.

Robert too was pleased that his expectations were still afloat. Here was a good-looking woman wearing a smart Laura Ashley dress and sporting a cute fascinator balanced incongruously on her beads and braids. There was clearly apprehension in her greeting. It didn't take long to see why.

From behind the folds of her dress a toddler of about two years old interrogated him with the big beautiful eyes.

'I'm sorry,' Ira mouthed across the room.

He walked quickly towards them and stopped a metre away.

'You two look great,' he said.

'I'm so sorry,' Ira repeated. 'Imogen's babysitter let me down at the last minute. Her auntie was taken into hospital and...'

'I know. You think you've got all the angles...'

Just then a child's voice rang out: 'Dad! Daddie, I've finished. Dad!'

Rob, half turned towards the exit and the loos, and then back to Ira. 'Sorry it's my son. It's Tom. I have to...'

Ira smiled behind her hand. 'I know,' she said. 'Go...! Go!'

Minutes later Robert was back with little Tom in tow. He and Imogen immediately locked in a staring match. Rob sat opposite Ira and conversation, rather like a twig in a stream, bubbled and halted as they explored points of interest.

There were some, but not that many. The topics were drying up as the tea and cakes disappeared. Some of the other tables had already changed cover twice.

Rob looked up from the crumbs on his plate and scanned the room with laser-like speed. Ira picked up on his alarm and for the same reason. Where were the children?

'Tommy?'

'Imogen?'

Both parents were out of their seats searching the room. Rob started towards the door. Then they heard the giggles. Ira deftly lifted a corner of the tablecloth to reveal two children, cross-legged beneath, covered in cream cake.

Obviously the two had formed an alliance and mounted a sortie on hands and knees to plunder the cake trolley.

They had successfully made a gateau getaway.

By now the whole tearoom knew of the heist. The waitress stood mentally adding up lost profits.

Rob passed a tenner from his wallet to her and gathered up his sticky miscreant.

'I think it's time we went.'

'Us too,' Ira said drawing little Imogen from beneath the table legs.

'Same time next week,' Rob asked?

'You could give me a ring,' she replied, and hid her smile behind her hand.

• • • • •

Dusty Old Book

I found an old dusty book in the library that has some interesting ideas. I always thought that people had evolved but that is not so – at least not according to the Bible. God did it all.

Christianity can be a bit of a pick-and-mix religion. Some people swallow the pudding whole while others chew over their favourite bits and discretely push the remainder to the side of their plates.

I don't want to get into the controversial aspects – bits about Jesus being his own father and coming back from the dead to live forever.... And all he asks is that we accept him as master... In return he will free us from an evil power that has infected us because a talking snake persuaded a woman, who was made from a rib, to eat a magic apple from an equally magic tree.

They put a mighty big stone in front of his burial cave to stop him getting out – but he was too powerful – of course.

It's quite a scary power too because normally rational people, people who run countries and who are in charge of armies and weapons capable of destroying the planet, say they have conversations with their invisible friend.

He gives them advice and forgives them when they go wrong. I think if you presented yourself at the gates of a mental hospital and told them you were hearing voices that told you what to do, then they would not allow you home to collect your pyjamas.

If you also confided that you believed in a whole collection of phenomena like speeches from burning bushes and invisible beings that keep a record of your good and bad deeds; a bit like Santa Claus does; you would certainly be on medication before nightfall.

Putting all that aside, there are some great tales in the bible, although after Genesis and God creating the world, to be honest, it goes downhill. God does some fantastic stuff. He creates the heavens and the firmament – only then does he create light. You might have thought he would have liked to have seen what he was doing – but no – he's God.

Anyway by time he gets to Noah, he estimates that the world is screwed up. He decides to wash it all away except for two of everything, or seven in the case of the clean animals. They will float in a boat that Noah has to build. God has tired himself out doing the planets and other big stuff, so he makes Noah build the ark himself.

The phone rings. Noah picks it up and says:

Hello... Yes hello... I'm sorry you're not very clear. Yes this is Noah...

Oh God, it's you.

What am I doing? As if you didn't know.

Planting a few vines. Yes...

Thought I'd try the Merlot this year.

Celebration?

Oh you remembered...

That's right – 500 today. I know... birthdays with a zero... Yes, they are always...

What...?

Yes... Yes I got the gift. Thank you. The Complete Practical Boat Builder. It's beautiful. The binding is...

Thank you again.

No, I'll treasure it.

That's not all...? You're having some lumber delivered?

It's what?

Sorry, you're breaking up.

Better – yes.

You were going through a tunnel...

So I'm to make space for...? Gopher wood.

No? Kopher wood? Yes... Bitumen. I see.

And I need this because...?

...Because you want me to build an 'ark'...

...And an ark is...?

Right...

You want a really big boat.

...At least 70 cubits.

I know I shouldn't ask... ...what's a cubit...?

Why don't we just stick to feet and inches – or... ...metres and – 'inches'?

Yes. OK. Sorry. Yes, you are the Lord my God.

Right...

Cubits it is then.

No I'd love to. Really. I've been looking for a project.

And fill it with animals? Two of each... ...or seven if they're clean...

And build a big cabin for poo because... ...we'll be at sea for a long time.

...A flood is coming?

...How do you know?

...You're sending it?

God, sometimes you have a perverse sense of humour.

Looking to spring clean, I see.

OK, just a couple of questions before I get started. The animals?

I know for a fact the ducks won't come. They won't. A flood isn't going to impress them.

...And do you really want the cockroaches?

...Put them where?

...In the room full of poo.' Good idea.

There may be a bit of a hold-up getting lions and tigers.

Why?

Well cast your mind back. You put them on different continents.

Get the Polar bears from Chester zoo... Yes, I could.

OK that might work.

Actually after the show you put on at Creation I'm surprised you need me to do all this.

I expect you were. I would have been too......completely. No I'm not just saying that.

No. I can't imagine what you were going through.

All I'm saying is...

Well you might want to think about taking something for your moods.

I don't know...People speak highly of Evening Primrose Oil.

Well one minute you are Love Eternal, and the next you are taking 3,000 prophets of Bale down to the brook to be slain.

No, I'm just saying...

Well, there are obvious inconsistencies.

I'm sure it isn't easy being in your position.

I'm not saying that.

Yes perhaps we should.

I will. I understand.

The deadline is a bit...

Haha! You love the sound of deadlines as they swoosh past. Hadn't heard that one before.

No, not at all.

...Before you can say twin outboards...

What?

Hello... Hello...? God?

Hello?

Anyone there?

It might interest you to know that in Petersberg, Kentucky, a $27 million Creationist Museum has opened, supporting the proposition that dinosaurs co-existed harmoniously in the Garden of Eden just 6,000 years ago. The displays include animatronic models of dinosaurs boarding Noah's Ark. They are expecting 250,000 visitors a year.

• • • • •

Melangell

I'm uncertain how we came to be there; what the process was; what the chain of synaptic blips was that put us in Cym Pennant that Sunday afternoon. There was an intuition we shared. There was some empathic trail we had scented and moved along.

Some months back on a whim I bought a small statuette of a hare. Then, she arrived in my life – this woman who knew me to my core. And I let go, and let her wash over me like a spring tide raking out the shingle on some desolate winter beach.

There is a truth carried in the air. You have to listen – to be ready to hear it. I think everyone hears it sometimes. It comes unexpectedly in quiet moments. It happens when you are walking or working. It comes from time to time when you have freed your consciousness. The gift can be anything: a phrase, an idea, a piece of music, an illumination.

Holding the figurine she recalled a tiny church, pre-Christian dedicated to the elusive hare. The hare is enshrined in cultures worldwide. My research told me it is so. It was revered in cultures diverse and estranged by geography and time; sometimes beloved, sometimes avoided – capricious, cunning, generous and fecund.

Independently we proposed to make pilgrimage to Melangell, but to make it together – a Sunday outing. Secretly we both anticipated some connection with the site. I can't say why. Why do lovers make the ties they do? Men and women ensnared by some small gift. Shared sayings become tiny bonds. It is as if we strive to secure the giant Gulliver with threads. We seek to wrap up love with gossamer strands.

I do remember crossing a bridge into the nape of the valley. The sense of being elsewhere was strong. We both felt it immediately. The landscape seemed a little different, the hues a little deeper, the hedgerows wilder and the trees more wayward. Stepping from the car I just needed to breath it in. I stood there and took in soulfuls of the green essence.

There was the tiny church dedicated to Melangell – two ancient standing stones commandeered as gateposts. Around the perimeter of the graveyard yew trees of immense age spread their shade.

'More than 2,000 years,' she said.

'As old as Christianity,' I replied.

'Yes. Perhaps older.'

She indicated a face of a hare in the bark of huge yew – as if she knew it would be there. I looked along the path to the church. It was well-cared for. The graveyard's orderliness was disturbing. Every headstone faced sunrise. When Judgement Day's the clarion call sounds the occupants will rise up in phalanx and parade to their happy day.

Inside, the church had pleasant appeal. Its simplicity was marked by benefactors plaques, engraved initials set in stone lest their gift be overlooked. Near the south door, the only door, was the oldest font I'd ever seen.

The stone might have been planted by some hero who had wrestled a plug of natural stone from arcadia, scooped out a hollow, then placed a simple wooded cover on top.

I sat for a while. We both sat for a while, and then continued dutifully anticlockwise around the knave, around the bones of the saint, for that is what Melangell is now.

The story is of She, the solitary holy woman with whom the pursued and terrified hare had sought shelter beneath her cloak.

Another couple entered the church and followed us around stopping to look at this and that. Then as I returned to my small meditation I became aware of another woman. Apparently she was the vicar and she busied herself with changing the flowers and the hymn numbers.

As she walked up the aisle towards me I looked up expecting a smile. It was if I were not there. It was almost unnatural how she avoided the opportunity for eye contact. So strange. So strange for a vicar in her own church not to welcome a visitor.

I indicated to my partner that I was going to sit outside. The afternoon sunshine was warm and the view of the hills as inspiring as the inside of the church. Across the graveyard a couple were working at something. Tidying a grave perhaps.

After a while Elaine joined me and we chatted about whatever lovers do. Quite soon we were joined by the couple from the graveyard. Inside it appeared that the vicar was holding a service on her own. We heard the church music. We heard her sermon but not her words. The couple were as friendly as the vicar was not.

They had an openess that was infectious. They spoke

warmly of their relatives buried within the churchyard; their relatives in the community. The soft Shropshire burr was as warm as buttered toast. They had been tidying a gravestone. He waved the shears towards the patch.

'Should we go in,' Elaine asked? 'I think she's all alone in there. It's so sad.'

'I can't sing,' the man said. 'No point in me going in. I can't sing.'

The woman just smiled her country smile. It was a face without guile or malice. At some point; and how the conversation got around to it I can't say; we were directed to the shade of the trees at the back of the church.

'That's were we used to go,' said the man, his face creased in smiles.

'Yes,' his wife said. 'It's nice and private there. No-one can see you.'

I thought we were talking about taking a leak. But afterwards when I thought about it I wondered if that was what they meant. His face was wreathed in smiles, full of fun and a little mischief. The sunlight lit the two of them there as if they had been drawn by some old master.

You see, when I walked to the rear of the church and stepped beneath the broad foliage of one of the trees, foliage that swept down to the ground, for a moment I felt as if I were beneath a cloak.

There was inside the church, solitary beauty – the bones of the saint dry and protected. But outside I was with life and the hares. And I was beneath the mantle of something far older. As we were about to drive away, the man trotted down the pathway towards us, shears in hand. He was still chuckling.

'I'll cut your hair,' he said to Elaine. 'Let me cut your

hair,' waving the shears towards the car's open window.

I expect people visit St Melangell for all manner of reasons. Some come for healing, some for Christian worship. However some come to honour an older religion – a religion in which hares and shears have another meaning, and the vibrance of life may be revealed, even to someone like me, from beneath the curtain of some ancient tree.

• • • • •

A Memorable Book

I'd like to tell you about a book that came to mean a lot to me. Sadly it is no longer in my possession but from time to time I look back with fondness and remember the impact it had on my life.

I came upon it quite by accident. I was wandering the byways near my home, a callow love-sick teenager, trying to find some purpose in my existence, and with a head stuffed with all the angst and romanticism a boy can have.

It was a bright summer's morning. It must have been in August because the barley had been garnered but the bales of straw were still standing in the field like strange Neolithic stones awaiting some pagan rite.

As I ruminated on life and the big 'why', I suddenly stumbled upon this discarded book in a hedgerow, and spurred by the gene of the young hunter-gatherer, I picked it up and carried it home for further perusal.

I have to tell you here and now that it was more of a pamphlet than a book and judging by the contents was something to do with the large hospital nearby.

Sadly I was unable to understand most of the text, not only because I surmised it was highly technical but also because it was in a foreign language which appeared to be Swedish, Danish or the like.

Nevertheless I could tell at first glance it was medical because of the graphic photographs displayed in the pages. Much of the content was of a gynaecological nature.

In the first section Cindy, I could make out that much, was displaying portions of her lower torso. She had generously removed her undergarments and was leaning across a snooker table – which was to hand. Using a snooker cue to support her leg, she thrust herself across the baize in an attempt to replace the pink on its spot – quite a stretch from where she was, I can tell you.

From her position I could immediately comprehend many of the mysteries of female anatomy as I am sure the student to whom this book previously belonged had also.

I quickly turned to the next section which showed Helga and Kirsten demonstrating how female friends can check each other for any unwelcome developments in their glandula mammaria – an essential practice for women I'm told.

Helga had raised her bolero top allowing Kirsten to palpate her breasts. It must have been painful as her head was thrown back and her mouth formed an anguished 'O' – something like a primal scream. Kirsten had helpfully removed her top altogether but must have been worried as Helga seemed to be using her breasts to prevent herself falling backwards. I have to say, the phrase, 'A dead heat in a Zeppelin race' came to mind but I pushed it quickly aside.

The centre section of the pamphlet targeted men. I quickly realised it was meant to be a test for penile erectile dysfunction. Juliet sat facing the back of a bamboo cane chair – which was to hand. Due to the humidity – there were beads of sweat meandering down her perfect body – she had removed every stitch and had captured that most complex female expression of vulnerability, desire and even a little wickedness. I knew quite quickly that I had passed the test, because my pants had become big at the front.

I recall moving with growing expectation to the next section which covered personal hygiene. Ingrid and Charlene sat in a large tub together demonstrating the environmentally-sound practice of sharing a bath. In a number of smaller stills they showed different soaping techniques, how to raise a really good lather, and what nipples look like after a brisk shower.

Finally, Jasmine portrayed the plight of the health service caused by lack of funds. She wore her nurse's uniform but it was clearly too small in every dimension. It also appeared as if her meagre wage would not allow her to buy the regulation underwear to go with it. Nevertheless she had done well with her make up and lip gloss which I imagine she must have borrowed from a rich patient – who was not to hand.

There were of course adverts at the rear for a selection of prosthetic devices for exploration, massage etc. These, while of passing interest, didn't capture my attention as had the preceding pages.

Over the coming weeks I referred to their captivating lessons many times.

Eventually, worn out by my studies, I decided to return my find to its former position in the hedgerow.

On passing by a week later the weather had broken, the bales had gone, and so had the book.

● ● ● ● ●

Bang You're Dead

Tim stood for a moment staring at the polished ash door. He balled his fist. The chewed fingernails of his right hand dug into the hefty palm then...he extended a split knuckle, gave a cursory knock and entered.

Behind the door there was little to identify it as a psychiatrist's consulting room. There was no ostentatious desk, no couch... Just a rather comfortable settee and deep armchair covered in a light-green floral drape. There were a few pieces of nice furniture, mostly Queen Anne, and some expensive-looking watercolours – mostly seascapes.

Tim raised two fingers and pointed them at John Hassop. "Bang your dead."

"Come in Tim." John gestured towards the settee. Tim walked forward, slipped off his army-issue parker and let it fall in a heap beside the settee. He settled himself in a corner of it, and crossed and uncrossed his old One Star trainers. He looked steadily out the large Georgian window to the bright green leaves of the plane trees in the courtyard.

It was several moments before John broke the silence. "Well Tim, how have you been since last time?"

Tim continued to study the rain-washed leaves now enjoying a fitfull relationship with the spring sunshine.

"Do you feel there is anything you would like to discuss this session?"

Tim rotated his head towards the psychiatrist and in measured tones repeated: "Bang you're dead. Didn't you hear me?" He slowly mimed pointing a pistol again and then returned to the view.

"Do you remember what we discussed last time? We did rather well."

"We talked about lots of things."

"I meant specifically what we said about your father."

"What?" Tim barked.

"We can talk about something else if you prefer."

"No...No, it's alright. You mean about my father being dead and everything?"

"Tell me what you remember."

"What!"

"About that morning."

"I loved him so much...respected him too."

"You loved him..."

"I told you, I loved him. He was a diamond geezer. We were always doing things together.

"What kind of things?

"Well, we went down the pub – and sometimes watched the races in Connoleys..."

"Connolleys is the bookies'?"

"Of course everyone knows Connolleys. You're not thick or something?"

"And that day...?"

"What..? ...I think you must be a bit of a dunce. Everyone in the street knows Conolleys."

"Were you going to the bookies that day, Tim?"

"No, I hadn't had my Gyro."

"So...?"

"Bang you're dead. Hahaha!"

"So...?"

"Bang you're dead..."

The room lapsed into silence broken only by a phone ringing in some distant office. Nature contrived to reflect a beam of sunlight from a patch of rain, and for a moment the far corner of the ceiling was illuminated by a kaleidoscope of moving light and colour.

Tim shifted in his seat. "Did you see that?"

John looked questioningly at him.

"The light was dancing on your roof. You don't notice what's going on around you, do you?"

"Did you argue?"

"Who?"

"Did you ever argue with your father?"

"Nah, we was great mates, me and him. Never a cross word."

"Last time you said there was dissent."

"What's that? 'Diss ent' working anymore."

"You told me you argued with your dad."

"Ok, well sometimes... Everybody does..."

"And he would beat you – savagely."

"Nah!"

"Tim, I have some pictures of you in Accident and Emergency. Your father was sent to jail for three months because of what he was doing to you – and your mother."

"She was no good. She deserved it."

"And you...?"

"I loved him. He was my dad."

"Did you love him when he beat you with a length of

hosepipe? Did you love him when he broke your nose. Did you love him when he locked you in the cellar for three days without any food or water?"

A cloud had moved across the sun and for a moment the room plummeted into a shabby ordinariness.

"No. I hated him."

"And that morning?"

Tim stared at the grimey rubber toes of his trainers.

"You were repeating something when they found you. Can you remember what it was?"

"Yes."

"What was it?"

"It's just a song. It's a song by the Llamas. Everyone sings it. Don't you know anything?"

"What was the song?"

"Bang your Dead, by the Llamas. You need to get out more doc. You're mingin' on youth culture you are.

"And your father?"

"...He was... He was dead. The old bugger was lying across the kitchen table with his face in his cornflakes."

"...And you were singing..."

The room brightened momentarily and then slid back into greyness. A squall moved in and thrashed on the window panes. Outside one could hear people scampering for cover.

Tim balled both fists and drew himself in. "I didn't know what to do. I didn't know – what – to do.

After a pause John exhaled and asked: "Would you like to end the session now?"

"I didn't mean to shoot him."

"I'm sorry, Tim, what did you say?"

"I'm sorry! I'm sorry, I'm sorry! Alright? I didn't mean to shoot him."

John Hassop looked squarely at him. "...Tim...you didn't shoot him." Tim turned and stared plaintively into the open face of the psychiatrist.

"We covered it at our last session, Tim."

"I didn't...?"

"Tim – you killed him with rat poison. It came from the cellar."

• • • • •

The Captain's Bar

He stepped from the solitude of the Festival Crowd into the solace of the Captain's Bar. They didn't see him. He was hard to spot. The room was full of writers, poets, musicians, artists – all offering their observations – the nuggets of truth they had scratched from life. They didn't see him.

One by one they stood and delivered words of beauty and truth in various measures – just like the barmen. No-one saw him nestled in the corner behind his beer. Why should they? He remained unexceptional.

He wanted to speak. He would have liked them to know his journey; what had carried him to the edge of his life. But more than that he needed a benison from their words. He wanted a reason to go on living for another day.

'Why can't I make my life better? Why can't I take joy in the good things which have happened to me?'

Someone spoke. It was the girl who organised the readings. He hadn't heard what she'd said. Then she was gone. Perhaps it was important. Too late to know.

He must focus. He would change. He resolved to. In his mind he rose and drifted to the stage to speak his poem in his special poetry voice.

Space chickens abducted me
Because I was a sinner
They trussed my arms behind my back
Just like our Christmas dinner.

Space chickens cooped me up
To meet their evil ends
I was just another Battery boy
In a universe of hens.

I was pecked, probed and basted
And stood upon a perch
Their beady corn-fed eyes on me
Foul deep space litter research

Space chickens implanted me
With electrodes in my brain
They said no-one would believe my tale
They'd think I'd gone insane

So when the mother henhouse
Rises slowly upon high
I'll stretch my neck, throw back my arms
And crow up to the sky.

It was a valid commentary, he thought, on the degenerating attitudes of people to their sustenance – of extra terrestrials and their opinion of us – to many things on which a college background might have inspired him to expound at length.

He could have talked about the sex he had with someone who was now a memory, and garnished it with adjectives of remorse. He could have talked about places and things which had no context for ordinary people.

But he would use his poetry voice, and his words would become meaningful. Yet no-one saw him. He had no doctorate. He had no poetry pamphlet. He had no website; no clip-on crowd...

This reverie was becoming fun. He laughed out loud and the person nearby turned to search for the cause. He must be careful not to appear crazy – going to the edge and shaking hands with the blackness wherein god hides, sheltering behind its depths.

Faustus knew the price. Don't follow me listener!

'A sound magician is a mighty god, and his dominion stretcheth as far as doth the mind of man.'

Don't follow me listener!

He saw himself float to the stage again.

'I have a poem. It's Haiku.'

Iko iko an nay. Jockomo feena ah na nay. Jockomo feena nay. No listen. It's called, 'Writer'.

In the blackness
Chained to a wall
If I stretch a little more
I might just touch you.

In the crystal of his mind he realised the bar as a microcosm of life. Here on this night everyone comprised the whole. Here were all the virtues and the sins. All held. All shared. Gathered in perfect ignorance. But the endgame of which he was part could not begin until he released the final sequence. They couldn't see it. They couldn't see him. He would let them sleep a little longer.

He rose to his feet and slipped past the speaker into the night – into the anonymity of the Festival crowd.

• • • • •

Puddle Jumping

The young woman scampered along the lakeside. A seasoned runner. She carried herself like the legendary Zola Budd, but with shoes, decent running shoes. The morning was bright; the air clear, the hour shortly after dawn.

In her mind she is running towards a clarity. Running from the fug. Emptying her life into a new future ahead, at the end of the trail. The trail is kissed by sprites, water, air, earth and sunfire. Along the path the alchemy occurs, re-tuning as if by magic her composite essence.

In the trees beside the lake there is more than sylvan poetry. Forest creatures have discovered an upturned hospital gurney and, as is their wont, have applied the experience gained from a seven-day course in lateral thinking. They are in the process of converting by the addition of a second-hand hyper-drive obtained in part exchange for three kilos of grade A conkers.

It's unfortunate because the patient from the gurney, 12-year-old Billy Sevens, is lying in a pile of deep leaf mould, flapping his arms like pectoral fins on a beached Minke whale.

'They must help,' he thinks, because he cannot speak. 'Someone must help me. I'm due in pre-op' in 47 minutes. I only came here to escape the rectal thermometer.

Stoat raises his whiskers to the wind and sniffs. He sniffs with discrimination. His sensory glands analysing the olfactive landscape.

'It's going to rain,' he confirms with satisfaction.

This is news to Billy Sevens who was convinced it would be dry enough for England to finish the Fourth Test.

Back at the car park Zola stretches, puts on her tracksuit, throws her running shoes in the boot, and drives home barefoot. Later she has to visit a friend's son in hospital.

Instinctively she removes one of the conkers from the M&S bag. Rubbing its perfect smoothness she puts it in her right-hand pocket – but then, after some cloudy thought migrates across her consciousness, transfers it to the left.

(After the style of Simon Armitage)

• • • • •

A Classic Consultation

A DIALOGUE

ACT SCENE I

THE SCENE OPENS IN UPPER ROOMS OF THE HOME OF JOSEPH WILLIAMSON. IT IS COMFORTABLY FURNISHED AND IN THE MANNER OF THE DAY HAS A LARGE FOUR-POSTER BED AND UPHOLSTERED CHAIRS.

JOSEPH WILLIAMSON: Not brought any of your fleas or ticks with you I trust?

DR WILLIAM HENRY DUNCAN: I have not, and I trust you have no sewer rats in your pocket.

WILLIAMSON: (Chuckles)

DUNCAN: There really is no point in my visits if you ignore my slightest direction. Should you choose to spend your days in some Orphean quest that is not my affair. However when it comes to your body, the body the good Lord gave you to do his work, I shall prevail.

WILLIAMSON: We'll see.

DUNCAN: If I do not then I promise you will pass from my care and enter that state you seem already to covet. Come bare your breast. Let me listen.

HE PRODUCES A LISTENING TRUMPET AND PLACES IT ON THE CHEST OF WILLIAMSON.

My God man you're drowning in your own fluids. Give up this digging. Pay some heed; for six months at the least.

WILLIAMSON: I need to be there. I have to direct the men. They must be told where to dig.

DUNCAN STANDS AND REPLACES THE INSTRUMENT IN HIS BAG. HE LOOKS AROUND THE ROOM.

DUNCAN: Do you ever let the day in? Sunlight truly is most healing. Some time in the sun would be most beneficial. (BEAT) Take time to visit your Virginian estates.

WILLIAMSON: What year is it Doctor?

DUNCAN: If I am not mistaken it is the year of our Lord 1839.

WILLAMSON: I have lived in this house for 34 years. I built it. I shared it with my dear Elizabeth. I built it in the same year you were born if I'm not mistaken. Should I now pursue some recreation to a lawless territory?(PAUSE) Besides I sold my estates years ago.

DUNCAN: I didn't know.

WILLIAMSON: Mr Wilberforce showed the way. (BEAT) Those pitiful beings... We treated the blacks worse than our animals, and we treated the Irish worse than the blacks. Negroes could cost 50 guineas – five for an Irish, the equivalent of 900 pounds of cotton. Negroes were durable and they weren't Catholic.

DUNCAN: This is not current news?

WILLIAMSON: No. I simply illustrate a theme that slavery is endemic, from beyond Moses. 'Necessity' is a vile word. It excuses every sin. (PAUSE)

I had occasion to be at the docks one day. A ship inbound had heavy passage and I went to see if the crop was spoilt. Because the master wanted to catch the tide, they were loading slaves at the stern as they unloaded my tobacco from the foredeck. I went to see, and I tell you Duncan it was like staring into hell. Under the monstrous iron grating there was every conceivable torment: fear, bewilderment, anger, pain, sickness – misery. Then I found myself looking into a face that bore none of these. His eyes had no hatred, no condemnation, They just asked a question.

DUNCAN: What question?

WILLIAMSON: It was no everyday thing. In that instant I had... I had a sense of everything – a sense of some great truth. As I was beguiled by that serene countenance framed by the iron grid, some eternal question had flown from him, to me. Now it was my question. He raised his head and I nodded my understanding. After holding my gaze he turned away to comfort someone – to comfort someone else.

DUNCAN: Thank God slavery is at an end.

WILLIAMSON: You think so. Tell that to the French and Portuguese.

DUNCAN: (PAUSE) You know they are now calling you The Mole of Edge Hill? Sir you cannot be unaware of the speculation on the miles of excavations you have created. Some say you meant to hold slaves in them – tobacco in, slaves out, but that you were thwarted by the Abolition Act.

WILLIAMSON: A man does not treat his horse as these poor creatures. The toll it took on Wilberforce... Declining health sucked him from Parliament. Praise be he lived long enough by just three days to see his act come law. But it was Nat Turner, the slave preacher, who showed me it was time to quit Virginia.

DUNCAN: I know little of him.

WILLIAMSON: Turner had a visitation from God. On February 12, 1831 an eclipse was seen in Virginia. What Turner saw was a black man's hand reaching across the sun. He saw it as a spur to rebellion. August 13 brought another phenomenum. The sun appeared a bluish green. On August 21 he led a two-day revolt slaughtering 60 whites. Some months later the militia caught him; hanged him... flayed him; quartered his body... (BEAT) He was hiding in a cave, (PAUSE) but you good doctor have your own crusade. I hear you intend we all should live much cleaner lives.

DUNCAN: Indeed. My healing talents are but a step from redundancy if people adhere to simple tenets. Outside they use the thoroughfairs like animals. There is no paving. There is no lighting. They urinate and defecate openly. The stench is ungodly and because of it cholera sits ever on our doorstep.

WILLIAMSON: At least we have water which is now quite good.

DUNCAN: But we have it for barely 30 minutes a day. I hold that it should be available to all, day or night.

WILLIAMSON: There would be a cost.

DUNCAN: Liverpool is wealthy. Who would begrudge payment to turn disease from his hearth.

WILLIAMSON: I hope the money is better spent than on that infirmary. It showed a lack of vision in its location, sited near lime kilns with their deadly night gasses, next door to a cemetery that reeks of decay. Really doctor, you seem determined to drive patients away.

DUNCAN: One better is planned. Let me say the present building has served our war veterans well enough. But this is something you already know. You scarcely turn a man away who looks for work. They tunnel and dig for miles on your whim, and not one seems to know the reason.

WILLIAMSON: (Chuckles) Perhaps not. Let me

tell you something, good doctor. Beneath this street, the street on which I built my home, there is a tunnel, not mine, yet in a way by my hand. The new railway has pushed through the sandstone, and who do you think led the teams? My men, my lads! Men who will dig 14 hours a day 'till their hands bleed if bid...

DUNCAN: Then that is the reason? That is what these secret tunnels are about? Not some refuge from Armaghedon; not a giant slave pen?

WILLIAMSON: That, dear doctor, is between me and my Maker.

FIVE SECOND FADE TO HALF

VOICE OVER: Joseph Williamson, known as the King of Edgehill, died the following year, 1840, aged 70. His housekeeper immedialtely disposed of all his possesions. No clue to his intentions regarding the miles of tunnels has been discovered.

Dr William Henry Duncan became the world's first Medical Officer – the first person to make the medical care of a city his practice. Repeatedly he underlined the link between poor housing, sanitation and the outbreak of typhus and smallpox.

He also set up another world first for Liverpool – a Borough Engineer. James Newlands was tasked with creating a modern integrated sewage system, a system 'excavated' beneath the city. The year was 1847.

FADE TO BLACK.

CURTAIN

· · · · ·

184

Blanked Out

'By 'eck! Tell me he's not dead.'

'I'm sorry Lester. I think he might just be.'

'What do we do now?'

'Well...'

'Check his pulse Ralph why don't you.'

'You check his pulse. You know I'm not fond of touching dead things – unless of course I'm cooking them.'

'This conversation's getting right weird.'

'We're not having a conversation, Lester. We are trying to deal with the prostrate body of our late friend and partner Harry P.'

Ralph got to his feet, stepped across the rug and threw himself into a fireside chair. 'Go on. You check his pulse if you're so keen.'

Lester looked around the room and picked up a copy of the Evening Standard which he rolled into a tube. He knelt by the body and pushed the tube gently into the crotch of the Late Harry P.'s elephant chords.

'Cootchy coo. Cootchy coo-oo!'

'Lester, what in god's name do you think you are doing?'

'I'm trying to rouse him. There is no way Harry would allow anyone to jiggle his testicles while whispering cootchy coo at him.'

Ralph sprang out of the armchair and returned to the body. 'For god's sake check his damn pulse. Here – like this.'

'I thought you didn't know how to do it?'

'Well, I've seen it on TV haven't I?'

'...Well?'

'He's dead.'

'I knew it.'

'Which leads us to the question of how to get the password?'

'To the Swiss account?'

'Exactly.'

'Maybe he wrote it down somewhere.'

'Well maybe he did, but we don't have all morning. Harry's cleaner comes in at eleven. That gives us 45 minutes...half an hour to be on the safe side. The fruits of two years' successful safe cracking...our seed money for the next big job...and our dear departed getaway man has pegged it on his own Hatchlou.'

'What?'

'It's a carpet Lester – a hand-woven carpet. The same carpet which will soon be saturated with poor Harry's body fluids.'

Ralph got from his knees and walked over to an etching. He read the title aloud to no-one in particular. "The World circa Elizabeth 1..." 'I can't believe he's done this to us. It's so untypical.'

'He surely would have tried to leave us a message if he could, Ralph.'

'That's 50 million euros sitting in an account in the land of poxy Toblerone and we, the rightful owners by default at least, can't get near it.'

Ralph looked desperately around the room for some clue as to where to start searching. Lester shoved both hands deep in his pockets and pulled a face. 'Should we call an ambulance?'

'It's a suspicious death, Lester. They police will be brought in, and for reasons only too obvious we cannot be involved.'

'What's going to happen when the cleaner finds him?'

'I imagine one of three things. She will scream or she will try CPR, or most likely she will have it away with that nice little bronze on the mantelpiece... She may of course do all three. Then she will make the phone call -- You know it's ironic. Who would have thought, after all the capers, that this would be the spot where Harry gave it all up.'

'The Hatchlou?'

'Exactly. Antique, double knotted, a joy for generations.'

'Are you sure it's not a Milas?'

'No it's not a bloody Milas, and when did you suddenly become an expert on oriental rugs?'

'I'm not.' Lester used his offended tone. 'I were watching Flog It on telly. They put up a Milas. It fetched a few thousand. Surprising really – it were threadbare.'

'Unscrupulous Istanbul vendors put their wares out in the street. It gives them that aged look. Then they take them home and let the donkey pee on them.'

'You don't say...' ...Ralph? There's a bit of paper sticking out of Harry P's top pocket.'

'Take a look.'

'By the way...'

'What?'

'What was the 'P' for?'

'What are you talking about?'

'The 'P' in Harry P... You knew him more than 30

years. What was the P for?'

'It stood for Pea. The 'P' stood for Pea like the vegetable.'

'I see.' Lester bent down and judiciously withdrew the slip of paper from the corpse's pocket. The focus of Ralph's attention swung from the room's contents to Lester. 'Well?'

'It seems to be a crossword clue. Harry was good on crosswords.'

'...I never knew that... What does it say?'

'"Blanked out. Cleanly from France, 11." And there are eleven dashes.'

'And Lester my dear old pal, if I remember there are eleven letters in the password to our account.'

'Don't look at me. Crosswords are a mystery.'

Ralph started tapping the back of his hand into his palm. In an effort to be helpful Lester said, 'Of course this could be nothing to do with it. If he did leave us a clue it could be in a book or taped to the back of a drawer. We could come back tonight and turn the place over properly'.

Ralph looked up slowly and with an air of pained disbelief said, 'That is not helpful. We shouldn't be anywhere near the flat after the body is found. So far we have done nothing wrong. It could be a trifle inconvenient to be discovered here but that's all. If we were to be found breaking and entering then the whole shebang could start to unravel. No, this has to be it. Harry would have kept something like this as a little party piece to try out on us.

'Ralph – it's nearly time for the cleaner.'

'Yes...Wait a minute...'

'I think I just heard the front door open downstairs... Ralph!'

'OK. OK...'

'Raaalph!'

'I've got it! Blanked out... Blank – blanc... In French, blanc is white, so come cleanly from France is washed, "Whitewashed" – eleven letters.

'Ralph, I can definitely hear someone on the stairs.'

'Lester, pull yourself together. It's high time we weren't here.'

• • • • •

Chidhood Holiday

I'm caught in a sliver of the afternoon; a piece of magic, a corner of a postcard from the past. There are sounds of children and holidaymakers and suddenly I am drawn into a time tunnel leading to a summer afternoon as a child.

For a moment I can smell fresh doughnuts sold at the Pleasure Beach. The sky is blue and the afternoon sun shines on my father's face. He is happy. Plainly he is happy. He smiles and looks at mum. He wears his tweed jacket with his shirt collar folded outside. Mum is smiling too. Her hair is dark and wavy and she is wearing a dress that sticks out at the hem and which has large pockets.

I too am wearing my collar open and outside my jacket; just like my dad. My little sister is eating ice-cream. It is an impossibly large cornet, and sooner or later mum will start rubbing at her dress as the swiftly melting confection drips over the unlicked side of the cone. She is wearing pink wire-frame spectacles with one lens obscured by varnish so her other eye works harder.

She has a squint caused by measles and had to go to hospital for an operation. Her measles erupted as we travelled to the seaside a previous year. We sat on a green Crosville double-decker bus on the bench seat by the stairs. My sister got redder and iller throughout the trip. Before we arrived at the seaside it looked like she had come down with something horrid. And indeed she had.

But today we weren't thinking of that. Her dress is sticking out like my mother's. It is due to layers of nylon petticoats beneath. Soon we will have tea and then come back to town to the Pavilion Theatre, or perhaps some other venue. Lord Rockingham's Eleven are on at the Pavilion and Cherry Wayner will be there playing organ as Red Price blows alto sax to their hit, 'Hoots Mon'. They will play encore after encore and I will clap so hard my hands hurt.

Earlier in the week I ventured up the main road from our holiday camp which was called Winkups and was the best, to another camp called Happy Days. It was seedier but interesting to visit. Happy Days had a café and at the back was a juke box. As a boy I could wander into places like this quite unnoticed. I had a cloak of invisibility that worked for long periods of time. I could go right up to the juke box and stand next to a Teddy Boy with drainpipe jeans and four-inch turnups, and he wouldn't even know I was there.

The hit played time after time was 'Teddy Bear'. I thought about choosing something myself when the Teddy boys and their girls moved from the Wurlitzer, but you only got two plays for a shilling. That was a lot of money just to hear a record. I would hang around for a while hoping to hear something I liked until I began to feel my invisibility wear off. Then I would slide quickly through the swing door and head back to my territory.

A good place to hear music was at the outdoor roller-skating rink in town. I think I learned to skate to Li'l Darlin' by the Diamonds. As I got better and could cross my feet over to go around corners I was afflicted by my invisibility. At this point I thought people might actually be admiring how well I did my feet crossing.

Strangely they were not.

My persistence, and my parents unwillingness to be my audience, led to their agreeing to my travelling to town by bus. I could go skating alone. I had my return fare and enough cash for a couple of turns.

I arrived at the camp as the sun was going down, hours later. My grandmother, face full of worry, had come looking for me. I told her I had lost my bus fare and had to walk back. It was a long hike; much further than I imagined.

The truth was, I had been lured into an amusement arcade by the slot machines. Once I had lost a little of my bus fare, I thought I might as well lose the lot, and I managed to do that quite quickly.

Now the aroma of candyfloss, doughnuts, toffee apples and hotdogs becomes swallowed by my present. I am engulfed by this new reality in which I live; but if I'm honest; and, at least in this tale, it seems that is in doubt; there remains with me a tinge of sadness at some innocence lost – some innocence rediscovered.

· · · · ·

Cortez the Killer

The dying strains of Neil Young's Cortez the Killer echoed around the empty hall. Phrases dripped – still dripped from the plaster walls. In the moment the disco ball seemed to hold, magically, the essence. Each line had a truth. I remember it. I can still remember it. The words: 'I still can't remember how or where I lost my way.'

The song spoke of a journey – the words held in suspension – blinking in the lattice light: 'He came dancing across the water with his galleons and guns.'

'I still can't remember how or where I lost my way'

We are all on a journey – many journeys – aren't we? Watching Oprah is a journey; family life is a journey. The problem is we invest in the outcome and so often we are disappointed. We control our actions – our motives may be pure but the result is not always what we expect.

It is the process that is important. Invest in the process and then no matter what the outcome we might still feel satisfied, still feel the journey was worthwhile.

The trouble is I still can't remember how or where I lost my way.

It shouldn't matter but Cortez is still inside my brain... 'What a killer,' Neil sang.

If in this timeless moment – this crystal of time, I could reconnect – report back to the great source of all things, ask directions, find out where I am, where I need to be and how to get there. Then perhaps I may have found that nothing was lost and something was gained in the halls of Montezuma.

• • • • •

Driving Thoughts

It was on the 15th – the 15th fairway... I'm pretty sure it was the 15th, and the Titleist 3 ball was my only consideration – my universe. In my hands my favourite driver with the boron shaft, whatever that is. My left hand was gloved. The 'V's made by my thumb and forefingers were aligned. I was ready for that critical moment when you take the club head slowly back until your spine corkscrews until it cracks. Then you allow the coiled vertebra to unwind, and reap the praise or consolation for a shot that migrates aproximately to the intended compass point.

Golf is a cruel game. Despite the handicap system it is an unfair game. It never seems reasonable to hit a dead ball. One has ample opportunity to rehearse the shot. One can pick any club in the bag. The ball is motionless. All one has to do is knock it from here to there in as few goes as possible. And the worst words you can hear are: 'Your turn again I think' – which to the layman, and in fact the player too, means you are still the one furthest from the pin.

On the tee, 'V's aligned I tried to clear my mind. I peered thoughtfully down the fairway, the most elevated on the course. The sky was angelic blue. The fairway had been well watered to save it from the merciless onslaught of Mediterannean sun. I looked for some Zen-like pasture in my mind where muscle memory could take over and allow my interfering consciousness to take a break. Too often had I floundered between overthinking the shot, or relinquishing control to the inept ingénue lurking within.

It was at this point a huge sunny smile crossed my face. The image of my former work mates, heads down, trying to meet a deadline in the UK filled my mind.

"What?" my partner asked.

"Oh nothing," I replied. "Just... Umh... Just thinking."

And as if by magic I slipped through a fissure gossamer-soft in my consiousness, and was driving home from work. I had been told, and I was prepared to believe it, that we are only fully aware of our driving for 25 per cent of the time. The robot in our head goes on automatic. Put in a slightly more startling light that means we only see one car in every four coming towards us. I sent a mental memo to self that I would attempt to be more attentive when next behind the wheel.

The thought led me to something I'd found while researching background for my novel. It seems that any decision we appear to make has already been made milliseconds ahead in our brain. This is perplexing if you prize that most human of attributes, free will. We appear only to have titular free will. We run our lives under licence. For example, you decide to stand. However somewhere the resolution was made in advance. Meanwhile you 'think' it, and take ownership as if it were willed by you.

I wonder what drives these thoughts. The idea of driving sent me drifting to, 'driving ambition', then across to what was, 'driving my values'.

Values, we all have them don't we? I'm sure I read that they are supported by a web of beliefs. Some beliefs are inherited, some learned, some acquired. They lead us to hold certain values. We may hold different beliefs, but share the same values. The odd part is that as strongly as we adhere to our values our beliefs aren't real. Beliefs aren't real. That's a big one.

If they were, they would be facts, I'm sure.

An elegant moment of no-thought followed – satorii; a footstep into eutopia. Then I crashed back into reality in time to see the Titleist 3 disappearing aproximately in the right direction.

I held the pose, hips rotated, club over my left shoulder just long enough for it to appear I knew what I was about.

As I walked off the tee the words: ' Your turn again, I think', carried on the wind. Golf is a cruel game.

· · · · ·

A Taste of Dickens

'It was the best of times, it was the worst of times... A Tale of Two Cities?'

'Annd...?'

'Charles Dickens.'

'I know that.'

'Of course. Absolutely one of the most famous opening lines of any novel in the English language.'

'The end's quite well known too. "It's a far, far better..."'

'"...Thing that I do." Yeh.'

'Exactly. And the point is...?'

'...What?'

'What put this in your head?'

'Oh, I was thinking about the code. The code they've uncovered.'

'The code? They?'

'They've cracked it. It's like the Da Vinci Code or the Bible only it's real.'

'S'excuse me could we just rewind a tad? You think there's some kind of hidden code in A Tale of Two Cities?

'It's obvious man when you see it. Like those fractal images.'

'What? You think it's the Masons or some kind of squinty-eyed, secret sect that has left clues in A Tale of Two Cities? At worst it's an episodic tale of obsessional cobbling juxtaposed with mistaken identity. There's been no speculation about the secret of the universe in its covers.'

'Listen, it was released in weekly episodes in Dickens' periodical prophetically called, 'All Year Round'. Only 31 episodes as it happens... ...so it only made it to October. However the method ensured best distribution among the acolytes. Time for it to disseminate among the ranks.'

'That can't be right. Dickens was against Freemasonry...'

'...No, no, no, no. He was just against the Freemasons of his day, who weren't living up to the ideals, the standards. You know?'

'Well not really man – like I mean it sounds a bit, 'Off the wall."

'The signs were there all the time. It's built into our language; hidden in everyday speech. Think about it. "What the Dickens", "Charlie is m'darling"; even, "Chase me Charlie, Chase me Charlie". You see?'

'...Well not really. Hardly seems conclusive.'

'Everything's in twos. The couples... The characters... Chocma and Binah... Kabalah. Sometimes they are alike, and sometimes opposing. Two cities. London and Paris like two lobes of the brain – left side and right. You see if you understand the codes in the book you will understand the brain. And if you understand the brain you will understand the planet, for the planet is one brain and we are like the neurons in that brain.'

'...That's pretty far-out shit man. I always imagined this tale was an enduring testimony to the best, and a searing critique of the worst of human nature. But like you're telling me it's like hidden clues to what makes everything tick?'

'Too right man.'

'You are full of it. I mean A Tale of Two Cities is, you know, a social critique. It's an exploration of the limits of human justice. I mean what is "justice" really? Is it murdering people who murder your family? Is it imprisoning people related to those people? When does justice start becoming... injustice?

'That is deep man, but you have to look further because that's just dressing.'

'Dressing? How can you call justice and social inequality dressing. This crap is using all the oxygen. Not another word. Take your theory and stuff it.'

'...You finished?'

'...Yes.'

'Certain?'

'...Yeh.'

'Then I have just one more thing to say: Character Madam Defarge, anagram Far Edge; Sydney Carton, anagram Tyranny Codes; Doctor Manette, anagram Random Octette; Charles Darnay, anagram Shed Carnal Ray. And to cap it all Marquis St. Evrémonde. This is plainly Everyman, or in French, Tous le Monde. Change Tous to the English numeral 'two' and it is clearly telling us the world is two. The two hemispheres of the brain.'

'You know something...?

'Pretty far out eh?'

'Listen genius I'll tell you about brains. In two million years the human brain nearly tripled in mass. It went from the 1¼lb brain of our ancestor Habilis to the 3lb dumpling that almost everyone has in his skull today. And it didn't just get bigger. It grew a new part. It got the frontal lobe, and particularly the pre-frontal cortex.

'Now ask yourself my friend why would evolution in a twinkling of its vast and omnipresent eye overhaul the whole skull to give us this new add-on – this cellular upgrade? Well, the pre-frontal cortex does many things, but one of the most important is that it's an experience simulator. Humans can have experiences in their heads before they actually try them out. It's a trick that our ancestors couldn't do, and no other animal can quite do. It's great. It's up there with language and opposable thumbs.

'Mr Kipling doesn't make cake with faggot and peas topping, and it's not because they mixed up an experimental batch, and then puked. It's because from one's exalted position in the comfy spot on the couch, you Mr Illuminatii can simulate that culinary experience in your head and say, "I don't think so". And I can also simulate this crap theory and say...'

'No, no, no, listen. Listen, it goes deeper and darker than the anagrams.'

'Yeh?'

'There's the cannibalism.'

'Come on!'

'The inspiration for Tale of Two Cities, and actually The Wreck of the Golden Mary and the play The Frozen Deep, was in fact the heroic friendship between explorers John Franklin and the surgeon John Richardson. Arctic exploration was really cool in Dickens' time.'

'The Arctic was cool?'

'It's precisely the same Franklin that Martin Carthy sang about on his second album. What's more, Dickens always, always slept facing north. He wrote all his great works facing north.'

'I remember the song. "I dreamed a dream and I thought it true concerning Franklin and his crew." Good song.'

'It is isn't it. Well, there was a suspicion... Strong suspicion actually. Well, Franklin died in unexplained circumstances looking for the North West Passage – three attempts. There was compelling evidence that Franklin's men, through desperation, resorted to cannibalism. Dickens wrote a piece in Household Words in 1854 defending his hero. It was nearly four whole years after the event. There was absolutely no evidence to support his contention that it was rabid eskimos what dun' it.

'No. Really?'

'I mean consider why would he do that?'

'I have no idea.'

'Because...'

'Listen man, I'm losing the will to live – hidden codes, planet brains, a bizarre friendship between two men, and cannibalism?'

'What do you mean bizarre friendship and cannibalism?'

'Cannibalism – come on!'

'No, I want to know, who we are talking about?'

'Franklin and Richardson, aren't we, and cannibalism? Who do you think we're...?'

I'm getting paranoid ...'

'Are you actually perhaps getting a bit hungry?'

'What? Hungry? Sure. Yeh. Maybe...'

· · · · ·

Five Stories on a Bus

LAPTOP

It was her I was sure. As the bus hiccupped through the morning bustle she was striding confidently ahead. I leaned as far as I dared across the 'orca' lady in the brown gabardine to peer through the streaked glass. She readjusted the top items in the shopping bag on her knee and quizzed me with a glance.

I was certain the girl in the street was the one sitting behind me in the coffee shop, tall, dark skinned, braided hair and beautiful almond eyes. And yes, she had my laptop on her shoulder.

I rose from my seat. It was instantly occupied by a standing passenger. The bus took a lurch and I grabbed for support. I could see the stop not far ahead. The bell rang. There was a hiss and the door folded back. I pushed for the exit and was quietly cursed by those in my way.

By now the girl had caught up with the bus and for the first time saw who was about to alight – me, owner of the laptop across her right shoulder.

I jumped for the pavement but had to readjust my landing as a tourist tried to climb onboard at the same moment. A crystal of pain unfolded as my right ankle collapsed. I hit the pavement with both hands, a knee and the certain knowledge that I wouldn't be walking properly for months.

As I looked up I saw she had stopped. There in a quiet pool of calm as she stared down at me. Then she smiled – it was a smile of triumph. The anguish on my face must have been obvious. With a flick of her braided hair disappeared into the crowd.

'Stop her,' I yelled. 'She has my laptop.'

But life had covered over the brief schism in time. Half the bus stop was fretting over me. The other half was stepping across my prostrate carcass to get a seat.

ME AND FAT BUTLER

Me and Fat Butler was on our way into town on the 47. He'd bin up west to see someone about a little somethin' for the weekend if ya get my meanin. We was feelin pretty chill'd cause it had all gone smooth like. He's starin out da window and I'm mindin my own, tryin to read the sports page over the shoulder of the geezer in front.

Suddenly, out the blue like, he says to me: "That piece what is in Newlands thinks you is sick."

"What?" I says. "What you talkin 'bout?"

"Na, sick like in cool. Ya know?"

"I know whats you mean," says I, "But I think you is 'aving a laugh. She is tasty enough, but I don't think we 'ave ever ad two words to say except, 'Here's da change.'"

"Well sis hangs out with that crowd down Boogie's. They all get bladdered on Fridays. Sis reckons Corinne would put out for you if you had enough savvy to ask 'er."

He emphasised her name so there was no mistakin.

"Fuck me."

"No, fuck 'er. She is top trim. I could do the roodys with 'er all nighty night.

"Fuck me."

"They is layin bets you won't 'ave the bottle."

Fuck. I was stunned. She was the kinda special piece you might 'ave a J. Arthur over if it had turned out to be another O' sole meo Saturday.

Fat Butler nudged me hard in the ribs. Our stop was next. Still dazed I monkeyed along the bus to where the driver could see me ready.

The bus stopped. The shelter was packed. They must a taken one off. The doors cluncked back and there I was, only starin' right into the face of Corinne herself.

We was barely a width apart. I remembered to close my mouth the moment Fat Butler pushed me hard to get off.

I didn't make the pavement, just the gutter. Corinne was smilin' down at me. As I looked up her long legs. I remember thinking, 'white'. She wears white.

ARMY

The bright spring air was exhilarating. I remember it vividly. We boarded the bus on that sparkling spring morning, and you could drink the air. My uniform was freshly pressed, my belongings stowed in my grip...

Everything was parade perfect. I stepped aboard the bus from the camp to my new freedom.

Two years five months and seventeen days in the hospitality of the Taliban was a lifetime's distance away now. It's locked in a box somewhere in my head. I'm not going to open that box ever. The debrief was a torment, reliving the dehumanising, monstrous journey while they wrote it all down.

You people... You people cannot imagine the degradation. You should not have to. You have grunts like me for stuff like that.

The army bus was grinding its way through the countryside, bringing us back to the town and our expectant families. I choked back the past and concentrated instead on the life-filled spring-green day the universe had given me.

There's a quietness to some spring mornings. It's like a Brigadoon awakening after a hundred years' sleep. The inhabitants are picking up the threads of what was happening all those years ago.

The bus pulled into the town square. There were flags and a band. Crowds of people had gathered. I didn't expect anything like it.

I grabbed my gear and searched the crowd for Helene. I paused on the bottom step. Then saw her but lost my footing as I stepped forward.

Helene's left hand was holding back a sob. Her right was holding the hand of a little girl As I picked myself up I saw she was beaming at me. I was looking into the smile of an angel. – my two-year-old daughter.

MAGIC BUS

In the sixties Ken Keasey's pranksters cavorted across America in a bus, The Magic Bus. It was sprayed with psychedelia and the refreshments, Koolade and OJ were liberally laced with Ousley's best lysergic acid.

For those of you who have never taken Acid it may be hard for you to understand what this was all about, but I will do my best to put it in a nutshell.

LSD is a mind-altering drug. It lifts the filters on the world. It lets you see behind the scenery. It connects you with the cosmos. It was the holy grail of drugs. And there were essentially two interpretations of the experience.

Dr Timothy Leary advocated taking a trip as it was known as a shortcut to a religious, "realisation". When you tripped you didn't just believe everything was connected, you knew. Understand, that because you took acid didn't mean you would 'trip'. That was when you went: 'Wow! Now I understand'.

Ken Keasey's Pranksters looked at a different side of things. They saw the whole setup, life etc, as a charade, a great cosmic joke. And the joke was on you, so you had better learn to laugh with it. People got on the bus, freaked out, and at some point climbed off. It gave rise to the saying, 'You are either on the bus or off the bus'. Do you see? There's no halfway.

In the mid 70s I got off the bus metaphorically speaking. You probably only need to trip once to get the message. My life on acid had become strangely repetitive. Yes, the fridge did always sing to me when I opened it. And I had ongoing back pain as my kidneys were forced to deal with all the substances coarsing through them.

So, somewhere around 1975 I stepped off the bus, tripped (pun intended) and fell at the feet of a young woman who seemed interested enough to smile at me. And if asked, yes I would do it all again, and maybe even use the same stop.

SAREE

It's remarkable how quickly you get used to travelling on one cheek when using public transport in India. What might look like a vacant seat, your seat, quickly becomes the shared space of two or more others, and sometimes their livestock.

You also learn to doze in that position too. Mile after endless, dusty, sunny mile needs to be accommodated. Your senses have been assaulted by the light, the colour, the odours and the noise. There is a jangling clamour in the cities, and the noise of dogs and dislocated voices elsewhere.

I roused myself as we entered the outskirts of Delhi. It is home to some 22 million people. The definition of Delhi and New Delhi is unclear so I make no apologies for avoiding the issue.

We had been churning through the traffic for at least 15 minutes. Either side was a shanty town. That anyone could call it home defies belief.

I decided to stop the bus and make my way to the hotel from here by rickshaw. It takes more courage than you imagine. When your rider decides he is going to cross a 12 lane highway, your chances of reaching the other side with your underwear in its current pristine state seem unlikely.

So I hopped off the bus and came a purler. As I dusted off my hands and knees, from out of a nearby hut stepped a young woman in a magnificent gold saree.

The juxtaposition of her with the background must

have made my jaw drop because she laughed, covered her mouth and performed a provocative glissando into the crowd.

· · · · ·

Lost for a Moment in the Fantasy

Lost for a moment in the fantasy of it all, my children stare up at the baubles illuminated by fairy lights. The colour of Christmas – new hope for the coming year – lest auld acquaintance be forgot and never brought to mind.

Rich cigar smoke, the smell of pine needles and tangerines; the change of lighting caused by festoons, balloons and holly, here, there and everywhere.

Strange parcels wrapped in brown paper with red sealing wax and white string, quickly taken up and ushered out of sight.

A surfeit of baking – mince pies, cakes, puddings... Sherry for all, even me when I was small, and a glass of port left by the fire for Santa Claus.

It was approaching – the darkest of nights that brought joy with the morning. Good food – big fires – and behind it all the fervent prayer that I would not be disappointed in the cold light of the morning.

Mr Lewis called – left behind a threepenny bit in brown paper for me to find. I liked him a lot – I don't know why. God bless us all. Please don't let me have to pretend that I got what I wanted – that I don't mind they forgot the batteries – that part of it is missing, or broken or intended for a five-year-old.

I love the carols and the choir and the dark mystery of it all. The bowls of nuts: brazils, uncrackable almonds, delicious hazels and the uncertain delicacy of dates in a box with a camel on the lid, maybe from the Holy Land.

It could snow tonight. That would make it ideal for

him to glide across the roofs and sneak in with crackling packages. Strange old jolly gentleman from some Scandinavian country, who sets out once a year to work the impossible miracle....

In the room where no-one goes stood the tree near a window where passers-by could see. And once in a while, curled and coloured wax candles were lit and we all stood around in the dark, prizing silver foil from chocolate toys lifted from its dry branches.

Staring – staring at our strange reflections in the illuminated baubles – lost for a moment in the fantasy of it all.

· · · · ·